THIS PUFFIN MODERN CLASSIC

belongs to

Some reviews of
Charlotte's Web

'An outstanding book for young children . . .
All the farmyard characters, human and animal,
are delightfully drawn: an adult reader will
admire and enjoy the pungent economy of phrase,
a child will feel that this is really how creatures do
think and behave' – *The Times Literary Supplement*

'The book has liveliness and felicity, tenderness and
unexpectedness, grace and humour, and praise of life,
and the good backbone of succinctness that only the
most highly imaginative stories seem to grow'
– *New York Times*

'There can never be too many reprints of
Charlotte's Web' – *Growing Point*

'No child should be without a copy' – Penelope Lively,
writing in the *Daily Mail*

Books by E. B. White

Charlotte's Web
Stuart Little
The Trumpet of the Swan

PUFFIN MODERN CLASSICS

CHARLOTTE'S
Web

E. B. White was born in Mount Vernon, New York, in 1899. He graduated from Cornell University in 1921, and after five or six years of trying many different sorts of jobs, he joined the staff of *New Yorker* magazine. The connection proved a happy one and resulted in a steady output of satirical sketches, poems and essays. In 1938 E. B. White moved to the country. He kept animals on his farm in Maine, and some of these creatures crept into his stories and books, such as those in *Charlotte's Web*, *Stuart Little* and *The Trumpet of the Swan*.

In 1970 he was awarded the Laura Ingalls Wilder Medal, an award given every five years to those authors who have 'made a substantial and lasting contribution to literature for children'. E. B. White received many other medals, as well as receiving honorary degrees from several colleges and universities. He died in 1985.

E. B. WHITE

CHARLOTTE'S *Web*

Illustrated by
Garth Williams

PUFFIN

PUFFIN BOOKS

Published by the Penguin Group
Penguin Books Ltd, 80 Strand, London WC2R 0RL, England
Penguin Group (USA) Inc., 375 Hudson Street, New York, New York 10014, USA
Penguin Group (Canada), 90 Eglinton Avenue East, Suite 700, Toronto, Ontario, Canada M4P 2Y3
(a division of Pearson Penguin Canada Inc.)
Penguin Ireland, 25 St Stephen's Green, Dublin 2, Ireland (a division of Penguin Books Ltd)
Penguin Group (Australia), 250 Camberwell Road, Camberwell, Victoria 3124, Australia
(a division of Pearson Australia Group Pty Ltd)
Penguin Books India Pvt Ltd, 11 Community Centre, Panchsheel Park, New Delhi – 110 017, India
Penguin Group (NZ), 67 Apollo Drive, Rosedale, North Shore 0632, New Zealand
(a division of Pearson New Zealand Ltd)
Penguin Books (South Africa) (Pty) Ltd, 24 Sturdee Avenue, Rosebank, Johannesburg 2196, South Africa

Penguin Books Ltd, Registered Offices: 80 Strand, London WC2R 0RL, England

puffinbooks.com

First published in Great Britain by Hamish Hamilton Children's Books 1952
Published in Puffin Books 1963
Published in Puffin Modern Classics 1993
This edition reissued 2010
6

Text copyright © E. B. White, 1952
Text copyright © renewed by E. B. White, 1980
Illustrations copyright © renewed by the Estate of Garth Williams, 1980
Introduction copyright © Julia Eccleshare, 1993

Set in 12/20 pt Book Antique
Made and printed in England by Clays Ltd, St Ives plc

British Library Cataloguing in Publication Data
A CIP catalogue record for this book is available from the British Library

ISBN: 978-0-141-32968-0

www.greenpenguin.co.uk

MIX
Paper from
responsible sources
FSC
www.fsc.org   FSC™ C018179

Penguin Books is committed to a sustainable
future for our business, our readers and our
planet. This book is made from paper certified
by the Forest Stewardship Council.

Introduction

by Julia Eccleshare
Puffin Modern Classics series editor

'Where's Papa going with that axe?'

Fern's dramatic challenge to her father begins a story of love and survival firmly based in the reality of farm life.

Saving the runty little piglet she calls Wilbur takes Fern into the heart of the farmyard. She watches over him as he grows – ironically only towards another death. But Wilbur is protected by others too. As Fern finds new delights, it is Charlotte, a large grey spider, who takes care of Wilbur.

First 'Some Pig' and then 'Terrific': those words mysteriously appearing in Charlotte's web have never lost their thrill. How did they get there? And how magical they must have looked! The story of the strong bond of friendship between Charlotte and Wilbur and their success in saving Wilbur's life create a sense of triumph matched by few other stories.

But while Wilbur lives, surviving to take care of Charlotte's babies, Charlotte must die. *Charlotte's Web* is also a story about how life changes and yet remains hopeful. As Charlotte dies, the barn is full of young – spiders, lambs and goslings. Everywhere there is renewal. Young and inexperienced, Wilbur despairs, but Fern, quietly sitting and watching the animals, grows up and understands.

As a child I loved the atmosphere in Zuckerman's barn. Fuelled by friendship, with comedy provided by the repetitive geese and the disagreeable rat, Templeton, its dusty, smelly atmosphere radiates security and contentment as well as privacy, something that children always want and adults often want to deny.

E. B. White was himself a farmer familiar with the feel of a farmyard and the interaction of the animals in it. He wrote *Charlotte's Web* as a way of exploring the enduring puzzle of farming – that taking care of sick animals is important emotionally, even though they will end up being slaughtered anyway.

Charlotte's Web was written more than fifty years ago and its message of hope and regeneration remains as pertinent as when it was written.

Contents

Chapter One
Before Breakfast

'Where's Papa going with that axe?' said Fern to her mother as they were setting the table for breakfast.

'Out to the hoghouse,' replied Mrs Arable. 'Some pigs were born last night.'

'I don't see why he needs an axe,' continued Fern, who was only eight.

'Well,' said her mother, 'one of the pigs is a runt. It's very small and weak, and it will never amount to anything. So your father has decided to do away with it.'

'Do *away* with it?' shrieked Fern. 'You mean *kill* it? Just because it's smaller than the others?'

Mrs Arable put a pitcher of cream on the

table. 'Don't yell, Fern!' she said. 'Your father is right. The pig would probably die anyway.'

Fern pushed a chair out of the way, and ran outdoors. The grass was wet and the earth smelled of springtime. Fern's sneakers were sopping by the time she caught up with her father.

'Please don't kill it!' she sobbed. 'It's unfair.'

Mr Arable stopped walking.

'Fern,' he said gently, 'you will have to learn to control yourself.'

'Control myself?' yelled Fern. 'This is a matter of life and death, and you talk about *controlling* myself.' Tears ran down her cheeks and she took hold of the axe and tried to pull it out of her father's hand.

'Fern,' said Mr Arable, 'I know more about raising a litter of pigs than you do. A weakling makes trouble. Now run along!'

'But it's unfair,' cried Fern. 'The pig couldn't help being born small, could it? If I had been

very small at birth, would you have killed *me*?'

Mr Arable smiled. 'Certainly not,' he said, looking down at his daughter with love. 'But this is different. A little girl is one thing, a little runty pig is another.'

'I see no difference,' replied Fern, still hanging on to the axe. 'This is the most terrible case of injustice I ever heard of.'

A queer look came over John Arable's face.

He seemed almost ready to cry himself.

'All right,' he said. 'You go back to the house and I will bring the runt when I come in. I'll let you raise it on a bottle, like a baby. Then you'll see what trouble a pig can be.'

When Mr Arable returned to the house half an hour later, he carried a carton under his arm. Fern was upstairs changing her sneakers. The kitchen table was set for breakfast, and the room smelt of coffee, bacon, damp plaster, and wood-smoke from the stove.

'Put it on her chair!' said Mrs Arable. Mr Arable set the carton down at Fern's place. Then he walked to the sink and washed his hands and dried them on the roller towel.

Fern came slowly down the stairs. Her eyes were red from crying. As she approached her chair, the carton wobbled, and there was a scratching noise. Fern looked at her father. Then she lifted the lid of the carton. There, inside, looking up at her, was the newborn pig. It was a white one. The morning light shone through its ears, turning them pink.

'He's yours,' said Mr Arable. 'Saved from an untimely death. And may the good Lord forgive me for this foolishness.'

Fern couldn't take her eyes off the tiny pig. 'Oh,' she whispered. 'Oh, *look* at him! He's absolutely perfect.'

She closed the carton carefully. First she kissed her father, then she kissed her mother. Then she opened the lid again, lifted the pig out, and held it against her cheek. At this moment her brother Avery came into the room. Avery was ten. He was heavily armed – an air rifle in one hand, a wooden dagger in the other.

'What's that?' he demanded. 'What's Fern got?'

'She's got a guest for breakfast,' said Mrs Arable. 'Wash your hands and face, Avery!'

'Let's see it!' said Avery, setting his gun down. 'You call that miserable thing a pig?

That's a *fine* specimen of a pig – it's no bigger than a white rat.'

'Wash up and eat your breakfast, Avery!' said his mother. 'The school bus will be along in half an hour.'

'Can I have a pig too, Pop?' asked Avery.

'No, I only distribute pigs to early risers,' said Mr Arable. 'Fern was up at daylight, trying to rid the world of injustice. As a result, she now has a pig. A small one, to be sure, but nevertheless a pig. It just shows what can happen if a person gets out of bed promptly. Let's eat!'

But Fern couldn't eat until her pig had had a drink of milk. Mrs Arable found a baby's nursing bottle and a rubber nipple. She poured warm milk into the bottle, fitted the nipple over the top, and handed it to Fern. 'Give him his breakfast!' she said.

A minute later, Fern was seated on the floor in the corner of the kitchen with her infant between her knees, teaching it to suck from the bottle. The pig, although tiny, had a good appetite and caught on quickly.

The school bus honked from the road.

'Run!' commanded Mrs Arable, taking the pig from Fern and slipping a doughnut into her hand. Avery grabbed his gun and another doughnut.

The children ran out to the road and climbed into the bus. Fern took no notice of the others in the bus. She just sat and stared out of the window, thinking what a blissful world it was and how lucky she was to have entire charge of a pig. By the time the bus reached school, Fern had named her pet, selecting the most beautiful name she could think of.

'Its name is Wilbur,' she whispered to herself.

She was still thinking about the pig when the teacher said: 'Fern, what is the capital of Pennsylvania?'

'Wilbur,' replied Fern, dreamily. The pupils giggled. Fern blushed.

Chapter Two
Wilbur

Fern loved Wilbur more than anything. She loved to stroke him, to feed him, to put him to bed. Every morning, as soon as she got up, she warmed his milk, tied his bib on, and held the bottle for him. Every afternoon, when the school bus stopped in front of her house, she jumped out and ran to the kitchen to fix another bottle for him. She fed him again at suppertime, and again just before going to bed. Mrs Arable gave him a feeding around noontime each day, when Fern was away in school. Wilbur loved his milk, and he was never happier than when Fern was warming up a bottle for him. He would stand and gaze up at her with adoring eyes.

For the first few days of his life, Wilbur was allowed to live in a box near the stove in the kitchen. Then, when Mrs Arable complained, he was moved to a bigger box in the woodshed. At two weeks of age, he was moved outdoors. It was apple-blossom time, and the days were getting warmer. Mr Arable fixed a small yard specially for Wilbur under an apple tree, and gave him a large wooden box full of straw, with a doorway cut in it so he could walk in and out as he pleased.

'Won't he be cold at night?' asked Fern.

'No,' said her father. 'You watch and see what he does.'

Carrying a bottle of milk, Fern sat down under the apple tree inside the yard. Wilbur ran to her and she held the bottle for him while he sucked. When he had finished the last drop, he grunted and walked sleepily into the box. Fern peered through the door. Wilbur was poking the straw with his snout. In a short time he had

dug a tunnel in
the straw. He crawled into
the tunnel and disappeared from sight,
completely covered with straw. Fern was
enchanted. It relieved her mind to know that
her baby would sleep covered up, and would
stay warm.

Every morning after breakfast, Wilbur
walked out to the road with Fern and waited
with her till the bus came. She would wave
good-bye to him, and he would stand and
watch the bus until it vanished round a turn.
While Fern was in school, Wilbur was shut up
inside his yard. But as soon as she got home in
the afternoon, she would take him out and he
would follow her round the place. If she went

into the house, Wilbur went too. If she went upstairs, Wilbur would wait at the bottom step until she came down again. If she took her doll for a walk in the doll carriage, Wilbur followed along. Sometimes, on these journeys, Wilbur would get tired, and Fern would pick him up and put him in the carriage alongside the doll. He liked this. And if he was *very* tired, he would close his eyes and go to sleep under the doll's blanket. He looked cute when his eyes were closed, because his lashes were so long. The doll would close her eyes, too, and Fern would wheel the carriage very slowly and smoothly so as not to wake her infants.

One warm afternoon, Fern and Avery put on bathing suits and went down to the brook for a swim. Wilbur tagged along at Fern's heels. When she waded into the brook, Wilbur waded in with her. He found the water quite cold – too cold for his liking. So while the children swam and played and splashed water at each other,

Wilbur amused himself in the mud along the edge of the brook, where it was warm and moist and delightfully sticky and oozy.

Every day was a happy day, and every night was peaceful.

Wilbur was what farmers call a spring pig, which simply means that he was born in springtime. When he was five weeks old, Mr Arable said he was now big enough to sell, and would have to be sold. Fern broke down and wept. But her father was firm about it.

Wilbur's appetite had increased; he was beginning to eat scraps of food in addition to milk. Mr Arable was not willing to provide for him any longer. He had already sold Wilbur's ten brothers and sisters.

'He's got to go, Fern,' he said. 'You have had your fun raising a baby pig, but Wilbur is not a baby any longer and he has got to be sold.'

'Call up the Zuckermans,' suggested Mrs Arable to Fern. 'Your Uncle Homer sometimes raises a pig. And if Wilbur goes there to live, you can walk down the road and visit him as often as you like.'

'How much money should I ask for him?' Fern wanted to know.

'Well,' said her father, 'he's a runt. Tell your Uncle Homer you've got a pig you'll sell for six dollars, and see what he says.'

It was soon arranged. Fern phoned and got her Aunt Edith, and her Aunt Edith hollered for Uncle Homer and Uncle Homer came in from the barn and talked to Fern. When he heard that the price was only six dollars, he said he would buy the pig. Next day Wilbur was taken from his home under the apple tree and went to live in a manure pile in the cellar of Zuckerman's barn.

Chapter Three
Escape

The barn was very large. It was very old. It smelled of hay and it smelled of manure. It smelled of the perspiration of tired horses and the wonderful sweet breath of patient cows. It often had a sort of peaceful smell – as though nothing bad could happen ever again in the world. It smelled of grain and of harness dressing and of axle grease and of rubber boots and of new rope. And whenever the cat was given a fishhead to eat, the barn would smell of fish. But mostly it smelled of hay, for there was always hay in the great loft up overhead. And there was always hay being pitched down to the cows and the horses and the sheep.

The barn was pleasantly warm in winter when the animals spent most of their time indoors, and it was pleasantly cool in summer when the big doors stood wide open to the breeze. The barn had stalls on the main floor for the work horses, tie-ups on the main floor for the cows, a sheepfold down below for the sheep, a pigpen down below for Wilbur, and it was full of all sorts of things that you find in barns: ladders, grindstones, pitch forks, monkey wrenches, scythes, lawn mowers, snow shovels, axe handles, milk pails, water buckets, empty grain sacks, and rusty rat traps. It was the kind of barn that swallows like to build their nests in. It was the kind of barn that children like to play in. And the whole thing was owned by Fern's uncle, Mr Homer L. Zuckerman.

Wilbur's new home was in the lower part of the barn, directly underneath the cows. Mr Zuckerman knew that a manure pile is a good place to keep a young pig. Pigs needed warmth,

and it was warm and comfortable down there in the barn cellar on the south side.

Fern came, almost every day, to visit him. She found an old milking stool that had been discarded, and she placed the stool in the sheepfold next to Wilbur's pen. Here she sat quietly during the long afternoons, thinking and listening and watching Wilbur. The sheep soon got to know her and trust her. So did the geese, who lived with the sheep. All the animals trusted her, she was so quiet and friendly. Mr Zuckerman did not allow her to take Wilbur out, and he did not allow her to get into the pigpen. But he told Fern that she could sit on the stool and watch Wilbur as long as she

wanted to. It made her happy just to be near the pig, and it made Wilbur happy to know that she was sitting there, right outside his pen. But he never had any fun – no walks, no rides, no swims.

One afternoon in June, when Wilbur was almost two months old, he wandered out into his small yard outside the barn. Fern had not arrived for her usual visit. Wilbur stood in the sun feeling lonely and bored.

'There's never anything to do round here,' he

thought. He walked slowly to his food trough and sniffed to see if anything had been overlooked at lunch. He found a small strip of potato skin and ate it. His back itched, so he leaned against the fence and rubbed against the boards. When he tired of this, he walked indoors, climbed to the top of the manure pile, and sat down. He didn't feel like going to sleep, he didn't feel like digging, he was tired of standing still, tired of lying down. 'I'm less than two months old and I'm tired of living,' he said. He walked out to the yard again.

'When I'm out here,' he said, 'there's no place to go but in. When I'm indoors, there's no place to go but out in the yard.'

'That's where you're wrong, my friend, my friend,' said a voice.

Wilbur looked through the fence and saw the goose standing there.

'You don't have to stay in that dirty-little dirty-little dirty-little yard,' said the goose, who talked rather fast. 'One of the boards is loose. Push on it, push-push-push on it, and come on out!'

'What?' said Wilbur. 'Say it slower!'

'At-at-at, at the risk of repeating myself,' said the goose, 'I suggest that you come on out. It's wonderful out here.'

'Did you say a board was loose?'

'That I did, that I did,' said the goose.

Wilbur walked up to the fence and saw that the goose was right – one board was loose. He put his head down, shut his eyes, and pushed. The board gave way. In a minute he had squeezed through the fence and was standing in the long grass outside his yard. The goose chuckled.

'How does it feel to be free?' she asked.

'I like it,' said Wilbur. 'That is, I guess I like it.' Actually, Wilbur felt queer to be outside his fence, with nothing between him and the big world.

'Where do you think I'd better go?'

'Anywhere you like, anywhere you like,' said the goose. 'Go down through the orchard, root up the sod! Go down through the garden, dig up the radishes! Root up everything! Eat grass! Look for corn! Look for oats! Run all over! Skip and dance, jump and prance! Go down through the orchard and stroll in the woods! The world is a wonderful place when you're young.'

'I can see that,' replied Wilbur. He gave a jump in the air, twirled, ran a few steps, stopped, looked all round, sniffed the smells of afternoon, and then set off walking down through the orchard. Pausing in the shade of an apple tree, he put his strong snout into the ground and began pushing, digging, and rooting. He felt very happy. He had ploughed up quite a piece of ground before anyone noticed him. Mrs Zuckerman was the first to see him. She saw him from the kitchen window, and she immediately shouted for the men.

'Ho-mer!' she cried. 'Pig's out! Lurvy! Pig's

out! Homer! Lurvy! Pig's out. He's down there under that apple tree.'

'Now the trouble starts,' thought Wilbur. 'Now I'll catch it.'

The goose heard the racket and she, too, started hollering. 'Run-run-run downhill, make for the woods, the woods!' she shouted to Wilbur. 'They'll never-never-never catch you in the woods.'

The cocker spaniel heard the commotion and he ran out from the barn to join in the chase. Mr Zuckerman heard, and he came out of the machine shed where he was mending a tool. Lurvy, the hired man, heard the noise and came up from the asparagus patch where he was pulling weeds. Everybody walked towards Wilbur and Wilbur didn't know what to do. The woods seemed a long way off, and anyway, he had never been down there in the woods, and wasn't sure he would like it.

'Get round behind him, Lurvy,' said Mr

Zuckerman, 'and drive him towards the barn! And take it easy – don't rush him! I'll go and get a bucket of slops.'

The news of Wilbur's escape spread rapidly among the animals on the place. Whenever any creature broke loose on Zuckerman's farm, the event was of great interest to the others. The goose shouted to the nearest cow that Wilbur was free, and soon all the cows knew. Then one of the cows told one of the sheep, and soon all the sheep knew. The lambs learned about it from their mothers. The horses, in their stalls in the barn, pricked up their ears when they heard the goose hollering; and soon the horses had caught on to what was happening. 'Wilbur's out,' they said. Every animal stirred its head and became excited to know that one of its friends had got free and was no longer penned up or tied fast.

Wilbur didn't know what to do or which way to run. It seemed as though everybody was after him. 'If this is what it's like to be free,' he thought, 'I believe I'd rather be penned up in my own yard.'

The cocker spaniel was sneaking up on him from one side, Lurvy the hired man was sneaking up on him from the other side. Mrs Zuckerman stood ready to head him off if he started for the garden, and now Mr Zuckerman was coming down towards him carrying a pail. 'This is really awful,' thought Wilbur. 'Why doesn't Fern come?' He began to cry.

The goose took command and began to give orders.

'Don't just stand there, Wilbur! Dodge about, dodge about!' cried the goose. 'Skip around, run towards me, slip in and out, in and out, in and out! Make for the woods! Twist and turn!'

The cocker spaniel sprang for Wilbur's hind leg. Wilbur jumped and ran. Lurvy reached out and grabbed. Mrs Zuckerman screamed at Lurvy. The goose cheered for Wilbur. Wilbur dodged between Lurvy's legs. Lurvy missed Wilbur and grabbed the spaniel instead. 'Nicely done, nicely done!' cried the goose. 'Try it again, try it again.'

'Run downhill!' suggested the cows.

'Run towards me!' yelled the gander.

'Run uphill!' cried the sheep.

'Turn and twist!' honked the goose.

'Jump and dance!' said the rooster.

'Look out for Lurvy!' called the cows.

'Look out for Zuckerman!' yelled the gander.

'Watch out for the dog!' cried the sheep.

'Listen to me, listen to me!' screamed the goose.

Poor Wilbur was dazed and frightened by this hullabaloo. He didn't like being the centre of all this fuss. He tried to follow the instructions his friends were giving him, but he couldn't run downhill and uphill at the same time, and he couldn't turn and twist when he was jumping and dancing, and he was crying so hard he could barely see anything that was happening. After all, Wilbur was a very young pig – not much more than a baby, really. He wished Fern were here to take him in her arms and comfort him. When he looked up and saw Mr Zuckerman standing quite close to him, holding a pail of warm slops, he felt relieved. He lifted his nose and sniffed. The smell was delicious – warm milk, potato skins, wheat middlings, toasted corn flakes, and a popover left from the Zuckermans' breakfast.

'Come, pig!' said Mr Zuckerman, tapping the pail. 'Come, pig!'

Wilbur took a step towards the pail.

'No-no-no!' said the goose. 'It's the old pail trick, Wilbur. Don't fall for it, don't fall for it! He's trying to lure you back into captivity-ivity. He's appealing to your stomach.'

Wilbur didn't care. The food smelled

appetizing. He took another step towards the pail.

'Pig, pig!' said Mr Zuckerman in a kind voice, and began walking slowly towards the barnyard, looking all about him innocently, as if he didn't know that a little white pig was following along behind him.

'You'll be sorry-sorry-sorry,' called the goose.

Wilbur didn't care. He kept walking towards the pail of slops.

'You'll miss your freedom,' honked the goose. 'An hour of freedom is worth a barrel of slops.'

Wilbur didn't care.

When Mr Zuckerman reached the pigpen, he climbed over the fence and poured the slops into the trough. Then he pulled the loose board away from the fence, so that there was a wide hole for Wilbur to walk through.

'Reconsider, reconsider!' cried the goose.

Wilbur paid no attention. He stepped

through the fence into his yard. He walked to the trough and took a long drink of slops, sucking in the milk hungrily and chewing the popover. It was good to be home again.

While Wilbur ate, Lurvy fetched a hammer and some eight-penny nails and nailed the board in place. Then he and Mr Zuckerman leaned lazily on the fence and Mr Zuckerman scratched Wilbur's back with a stick.

'He's quite a pig,' said Lurvy.

'Yes, he'll make a good pig,' said Mr Zuckerman.

Wilbur heard the words of praise. He felt the warm milk inside his stomach. He felt the pleasant rubbing of the stick along his itchy back. He felt peaceful and happy and sleepy. This had been a tiring afternoon. It was still only about four o'clock but Wilbur was ready for bed.

'I'm really too young to go out into the world alone,' he thought as he lay down.

Chapter Four
Loneliness

The next day was rainy and dark. Rain fell on the roof of the barn and dripped steadily from the eaves. Rain fell in the barnyard and ran in crooked courses down into the lane where thistles and pigweed grew. Rain spattered against Mrs Zuckerman's kitchen windows and came gushing out of the downspouts. Rain fell on the backs of the sheep as they grazed in the meadow. When the sheep tired of standing in the rain, they walked slowly up the lane and into the fold.

Rain upset Wilbur's plans. Wilbur had planned to go out, this day, and dig a new hole in his yard. He had other plans, too. His plans for the day went something like this:

Breakfast at six-thirty. Skim milk, crusts, middlings, bits of doughnuts, wheat cakes with drops of maple syrup sticking to them, potato skins, left-over custard pudding with raisins, and bits of Shredded Wheat.

Breakfast would be finished at seven.

From seven to eight, Wilbur planned to have a talk with Templeton, the rat that lived under his trough. Talking with Templeton was not the most interesting occupation in the world but it was better than nothing.

From eight to nine, Wilbur planned to take a nap outdoors in the sun.

From nine to eleven, he planned to dig a hole, or trench, and possibly find something good to eat buried in the dirt.

From eleven to twelve, he planned to stand still and watch flies on the boards, watch bees in the clover, and watch swallows in the air.

Twelve o'clock – lunchtime. Middlings,

warm water, apple parings, meat gravy, carrot scrapings, meat scraps, stale hominy, and the wrapper off a package of cheese. Lunch would be over at one.

From one to two, Wilbur planned to sleep.

From two to three, he planned to scratch itchy places by rubbing against the fence.

From three to four, he planned to stand perfectly still and think of what it was like to be alive, and to wait for Fern.

At four would come supper. Skim milk, provender left-over sandwich from Lurvy's lunchbox, prune skins, a morsel of this, a bit of that, fried potatoes, marmalade drippings, a little more of this, a little more of that, a piece of baked apple, a scrap of upside-down cake.

Wilbur had gone to sleep thinking about these plans. He awoke at six and saw the rain, and it seemed as though he couldn't bear it.

'I get everything all beautifully planned out and it has to go and rain,' he said.

For a while he stood gloomily indoors. Then he walked to the door and looked out. Drops of rain struck his face. His yard was cold and wet. His trough had an inch of rain water in it. Templeton was nowhere to be seen.

'Are you out there, Templeton?' called Wilbur. There was no answer. Suddenly Wilbur felt lonely and friendless.

'One day just like another,' he groaned. 'I'm very young, I have no real friend here in the barn, it's going to rain all morning and all afternoon, and Fern won't come in such bad weather. Oh, *honestly*!' And Wilbur was crying again, for the second time in two days.

At six-thirty Wilbur heard the banging of a pail. Lurvy was standing outside in the rain, stirring up breakfast.

'C'mon, pig!' said Lurvy.

Wilbur did not budge. Lurvy dumped the slops, scraped the pail, and walked away. He noticed that something was wrong with the pig.

Wilbur didn't want food, he wanted love. He wanted a friend – someone who would play with him. He mentioned this to the goose, who was sitting quietly in a corner of the sheepfold.

'Will you come over and play with me?' he asked.

'Sorry, sonny, sorry,' said the goose. 'I'm sitting-sitting on my eggs. Eight of them. Got to keep them toasty-oasty-oasty warm. I have to stay right here, I'm no flibberty-ibberty-gibbet. I do not play when there are eggs to hatch. I'm expecting goslings.'

'Well, I didn't think you were expecting woodpeckers,' said Wilbur bitterly.

Wilbur next tried one of the lambs.

'Will you please play with me?' he asked.

'Certainly not,' said the lamb. 'In the first place, I cannot get into your pen, as I am not old enough to jump over the fence. In the second place, I am not interested in pigs. Pigs mean less than nothing to me.'

'What do you mean, *less* than nothing?' replied Wilbur. 'I don't think there is any such thing as less than nothing. Nothing is absolutely the limit of nothingness. It's the lowest you can go. It's the end of the line. How can something

be less than nothing? If there were something that was less than nothing, then nothing would not be nothing, it would be something – even though it's just a very little bit of something. But if nothing is nothing, then nothing has nothing that is less than it is.'

'Oh, be quiet!' said the lamb. 'Go play by yourself ! I don't play with pigs.'

Sadly, Wilbur lay down and listened to the rain. Soon he saw the rat climbing down a slanting board that he used as a stairway.

'Will you play with me, Templeton?' asked Wilbur.

'Play?' said Templeton, twirling his whiskers. 'Play? I hardly know the meaning of the word.'

'Well,' said Wilbur, 'it means to have fun, to frolic, to run and skip and make merry.'

'I never do those things if I can avoid them,' replied the rat, sourly. 'I prefer to spend my time eating, gnawing, spying, and hiding. I am a glutton but not a merrymaker. Right now I am on my way to your trough to eat your breakfast, since you haven't got sense enough to eat it yourself.' And Templeton, the rat, crept stealthily along the wall and disappeared into a private tunnel that he had dug between the door and the trough in Wilbur's yard. Templeton was a crafty rat, and he had things pretty much his own way. The tunnel was an example of his skill and cunning. The tunnel enabled him to get from the barn to his hiding-place under the pig trough without coming out into the open. He had tunnels and runways all over Mr Zuckerman's farm and could get from one place to another without being seen. Usually he slept during the daytime and was abroad only after dark.

Wilbur watched him disappear into his tunnel. In a moment he saw the rat's sharp nose poke out from underneath the wooden trough. Cautiously Templeton pulled himself up over the edge of the trough. This was almost more than Wilbur could stand: on this dreary, rainy day to see his breakfast being eaten by somebody else. He knew Templeton was getting soaked, out there in the pouring rain,

but even that didn't comfort him. Friendless, dejected, and hungry, he threw himself down in the manure and sobbed.

Late that afternoon, Lurvy went to Mr Zuckerman. 'I think there's something wrong with that pig of yours. He hasn't touched his food.'

'Give him two spoonfuls of sulphur and a little molasses,' said Mr Zuckerman.

Wilbur couldn't believe what was happening to him when Lurvy caught him and forced the medicine down his throat. This was certainly the worst day of his life. He didn't know whether he could endure the awful loneliness any more.

Darkness settled over everything. Soon there

were only shadows and the noises of the sheep chewing their cuds, and occasionally the rattle of a cow-chain up overhead. You can imagine Wilbur's surprise when, out of the darkness, came a small voice he had never heard before. It sounded rather thin, but pleasant. 'Do you want a friend, Wilbur?' it said. 'I'll be a friend to you. I've watched you all day and I like you.'

'But I can't see you,' said Wilbur, jumping to his feet. 'Where are you? And *who* are you?'

'I'm right up here,' said the voice. 'Go to sleep. You'll see me in the morning.'

Chapter Five
Charlotte

The night seemed long. Wilbur's stomach was empty and his mind was full. And when your stomach is empty and your mind is full, it's always hard to sleep.

A dozen times during the night Wilbur woke and stared into the blackness, listening to the sounds and trying to figure out what time it was. A barn is never perfectly quiet. Even at midnight there is usually something stirring.

The first time he woke, he heard Templeton gnawing a hole in the grain bin. Templeton's teeth scraped loudly against the wood and made quite a racket. 'That crazy rat!' thought

Wilbur. 'Why does he have to stay up all night, grinding his clashers and destroying people's property? Why can't he go to sleep, like any decent animal?'

The second time Wilbur woke, he heard the goose turning on her nest and chuckling to herself.

'What time is it?' whispered Wilbur to the goose.

'Probably-obably-obably about half past eleven,' said the goose. 'Why aren't you asleep, Wilbur?'

'Too many things on my mind,' said Wilbur.

'Well,' said the goose, 'that's not *my* trouble. I have nothing at all on my mind, but I've too many things under my behind. Have you ever tried to sleep while sitting on eight eggs?'

'No,' replied Wilbur. 'I suppose it is uncomfortable. How long does it take a goose egg to hatch?'

'Approximately-oximately thirty days, all

told,' answered the goose. 'But I cheat a little. On warm afternoons, I just pull a little straw over the eggs and go out for a walk.'

Wilbur yawned and went back to sleep. In his dreams he heard again the voice saying, 'I'll be a friend to you. Go to sleep – you'll see me in the morning.'

About half an hour before dawn, Wilbur woke and listened. The barn was still dark. The sheep lay motionless. Even the goose was quiet. Overhead, on the main floor, nothing stirred: the cows were resting, the horses dozed. Templeton had quit work and gone off somewhere on an errand. The only sound was a slight scraping noise from the rooftop, where the weather-vane swung back and forth. Wilbur loved the barn when it was like this – calm and quiet, waiting for light.

'Day is almost here,' he thought.

Through a small window, a faint gleam appeared. One by one the stars went out.

Wilbur could see the goose a few feet away. She sat with head tucked under a wing. Then he could see the sheep and the lambs. The sky lightened.

'Oh, beautiful day, it is here at last! Today I shall find my friend.'

Wilbur looked everywhere. He searched his pen thoroughly. He examined the window ledge, stared up at the ceiling. But he saw nothing new. Finally he decided he would have to speak up. He hated to break the lovely stillness of dawn by using his voice, but he couldn't think of any other way to locate the mysterious new friend who was nowhere to be seen. So Wilbur cleared his throat.

'Attention, please!' he said in a loud, firm voice. 'Will the party who addressed me at bedtime last night kindly make himself or herself known by giving an appropriate sign or signal!'

Wilbur paused and listened. All the other

animals lifted their heads and stared at him. Wilbur blushed. But he was determined to get in touch with his unknown friend.

'Attention, please!' he said. 'I will repeat the message. Will the party who addressed me at bedtime last night kindly speak up. Please tell me where you are, if you are my friend!'

The sheep looked at each other in disgust.

'Stop your nonsense, Wilbur!' said the oldest sheep. 'If you have a new friend here, you are probably disturbing his rest; and the quickest way to spoil a friendship is to wake somebody up in the morning before he is ready. How can you be sure your friend is an early riser?'

'I beg everyone's pardon,' whispered Wilbur. 'I didn't mean to be objectionable.'

He lay down meekly in the manure, facing the door. He did not know it, but his friend was very near. And the old sheep was right – the friend was still asleep.

Soon Lurvy appeared with slops for

breakfast. Wilbur rushed out, ate everything in a hurry, and licked the trough. The sheep moved off down the lane, the gander waddled along behind them, pulling grass. And then, just as Wilbur was settling down for his morning nap, he heard again the thin voice that had addressed him the night before.

'Salutations!' said the voice.

Wilbur jumped to his feet. 'Salu-*what*?' he cried.

'Salutations!' repeated the voice.

'What are *they*, and where are *you*?' screamed Wilbur. 'Please, *please*, tell me where you are. And what are salutations?'

'Salutations are greetings,' said the voice. 'When I say "salutations", it's just my fancy way of saying hello or good morning. Actually, it's a silly expression, and I am surprised that I used it at all. As for my whereabouts, that's easy. Look up here in the corner of the doorway! Here I am. Look, I'm waving!'

At last Wilbur saw the creature that had spoken to him in such a kindly way. Stretched across the upper part of the doorway was a big spider's web, and hanging from the top of the web, head down, was a large grey spider. She was about the size of a gum-drop. She had eight legs, and she was waving one of them at Wilbur in friendly greeting. 'See me now?' she asked.

'Oh, yes indeed,' said Wilbur. 'Yes indeed! How are you? Good morning! Salutations! Very pleased to meet you. What is your name, please? May I have your name?'

'My name,' said the spider, 'is Charlotte.'

'Charlotte what?' asked Wilbur, eagerly.

'Charlotte A. Cavatica. But just call me Charlotte.'

'I think you're beautiful,' said Wilbur.

'Well, I *am* pretty,' replied Charlotte. 'There's no denying that. Almost all spiders are rather nice-looking. I'm not as flashy as some, but I'll

do. I wish I could see you, Wilbur, as clearly as you can see me.'

'Why can't you?' asked the pig. 'I'm right here.'

'Yes, but I'm near-sighted,' replied Charlotte. 'I've always been dreadfully near-sighted. It's good in some ways, not so good in others. Watch me wrap up this fly.'

A fly that had been crawling along Wilbur's trough had flown up and blundered into the lower part of Charlotte's web and was tangled in the sticky threads. The fly was beating its wings furiously trying to break loose and free itself.

'First,' said Charlotte, 'I dive at him.' She plunged head-first towards the fly. As she dropped, a tiny silken thread unwound from her rear end.

'Next, I wrap him up.' She grabbed the fly, threw a few jets of silk round it, and rolled it over and over, wrapping it so that it couldn't move. Wilbur watched in horror. He could hardly believe what he was seeing, and although he detested flies he was sorry for this one.

'There!' said Charlotte. 'Now I knock him out, so he'll be more comfortable.' She bit the fly. 'He can't feel a thing now,' she remarked. 'He'll make a perfect breakfast for me.'

'You mean you eat flies?' gasped Wilbur.

'Certainly. Flies, bugs, grasshoppers, choice beetles, moths, butterflies, tasty cockroaches, gnats, midgets, daddy-long-legs, centipedes, mosquitoes, crickets – anything that is careless enough to get caught in my web. I have to live, don't I?'

'Why, yes, of course,' said Wilbur. 'Do they taste good?'

'Delicious. Of course, I don't really eat them. I drink them – drink their blood. I love blood,' said Charlotte, and her pleasant, thin voice

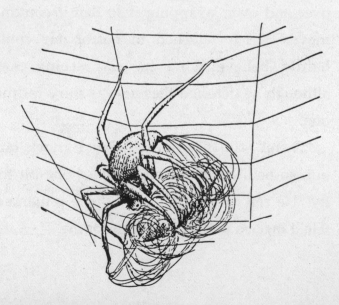

grew even thinner and more pleasant.

'Don't say that!' groaned Wilbur. 'Please don't say things like that!'

'Why not? It's true, and I have to say what is true. I am not entirely happy about my diet of flies and bugs, but it's the way I'm made. A spider has to pick up a living somehow or other, and I happen to be a trapper. I just naturally build a web and trap flies and other insects. My mother was a trapper before me. Her mother was a trapper before her. All our family have been trappers. Way back for thousands and thousands of years we spiders have been laying for flies and bugs.'

'It's a miserable inheritance,' said Wilbur, gloomily. He was sad because his new friend was so bloodthirsty.

'Yes, it is,' agreed Charlotte. 'But I can't help it. I don't know how the first spider in the early days of the world happened to think up this fancy idea of spinning a web, but she did, and it was clever of her, too. And since then, all of us spiders have had to work the same trick. It's not a bad pitch, on the whole.'

'It's cruel,' replied Wilbur, who did not intend to be argued out of his position.

'Well, *you* can't talk,' said Charlotte. '*You* have your meals brought to you in a pail. Nobody feeds me. I have to get my own living. I live by my wits. I have to be sharp and clever, lest I go hungry. I have to think things out, catch what I can, take what comes. And it just so happens, my friend, that what comes is flies and insects and bugs. And *further*more,' said Charlotte, shaking one of her legs, 'do you realize that if I didn't catch bugs and eat them, bugs would increase and multiply and get so numerous that they'd destroy the earth, wipe out everything?'

'Really?' said Wilbur. 'I wouldn't want *that* to happen. Perhaps your web is a good thing after all.'

The goose had been listening to this conversation and chuckling to herself. 'There are a lot of things Wilbur doesn't know about life,' she thought. 'He's really a very innocent little pig. He doesn't even know what's going to happen to him around Christmastime; he has no idea that Mr Zuckerman and Lurvy are plotting to kill him.' And the goose raised herself a bit and poked her eggs a little farther under her so that they would receive the full heat from her warm body and soft feathers.

Charlotte stood quietly over the fly, preparing to eat it. Wilbur lay down and closed his eyes. He was tired from his wakeful night and from the excitement of meeting someone for the first time. A breeze brought him the smell of clover – the sweet-smelling world beyond his fence. 'Well,' he thought, 'I've got a new friend, all right. But what a gamble friendship is! Charlotte is fierce, brutal, scheming, bloodthirsty – everything I don't like.

How can I learn to like her, even though she is pretty and, of course, clever?'

Wilbur was merely suffering the doubts and fears that often go with finding a new friend. In good time he was to discover that he was mistaken about Charlotte. Underneath her rather bold and cruel exterior, she had a kind heart, and she was to prove loyal and true to the very end.

Chapter Six
Summer Days

The early summer days on a farm are the happiest and fairest days of the year. Lilacs bloom and make the air sweet, and then fade. Apple blossoms come with the lilacs, and the bees visit round among the apple trees. The days grow warm and soft. School ends, and children have time to play and to fish for trout in the brook. Avery often brought a trout home in his pocket, warm and stiff and ready to be fried for supper.

Now that school was over, Fern visited the barn almost every day, to sit quietly on her stool. The animals treated her as an equal. The sheep lay calmly at her feet.

Around the first of July, the work horses were hitched to the mowing machine, and Mr Zuckerman climbed into the seat and drove into the field. All morning you could hear the rattle of the machine as it went round and round, while the tall grass fell down behind the cutter bay in long green swathes. Next day, if there was no thunder shower, all hands would help rake and pitch and load, and the hay would be carried to the barn in the high hay wagon, with Fern and Avery riding at the top of the load. Then the hay would be hoisted, sweet and warm, into the big loft, until the whole barn seemed like a wonderful bed of timothy and clover. It was fine to jump in, and perfect to hide in. And sometimes Avery would find a little grass snake in the hay, and would add it to the other things in his pocket.

Early summer days are a jubilee time for birds. In the fields, around the house, in the barn, in the woods, in the swamp – everywhere love and songs and nests and eggs. From the edge of the woods, the white-throated sparrow (which must come all the way from Boston) calls, 'Oh, Peabody, Peabody, Peabody!' On an apple bough, the phoebe teeters and wags its tail and says, 'Phoebe, phoe-bee!' The song sparrow, who knows how brief and lovely life is, says, 'Sweet, sweet, sweet interlude; sweet, sweet, sweet interlude.' If you enter the barn, the swallows swoop down from their nests and scold. 'Cheeky, cheeky!' they say.

In early summer there are plenty of things for a child to eat and drink and suck and chew. Dandelion stems are full of milk, clover heads are loaded with nectar, the Frigidaire is full of ice-cold drinks. Everywhere you look is life; even the little ball of spit on the weed stalk, if you poke it apart, has a green worm inside it. And on the underside of the leaf of the potato vine are the bright orange eggs of the potato bug.

It was on a day in early summer that the goose eggs hatched. This was an important event in the barn cellar. Fern was there, sitting on her stool, when it happened.

Except for the goose herself, Charlotte was the first to know that the goslings had at last arrived. The goose knew a day in advance that they were coming – she could hear their weak voices calling from inside the egg. She knew that they were in a desperately cramped position inside the shell and were most anxious to break through and get out. So she sat quite still, and talked less than usual.

When the first gosling poked its grey-green head through the goose's feathers and looked around, Charlotte spied it and made the announcement.

'I am sure,' she said, 'that every one of us here will be gratified to learn that after four weeks of unremitting effort and patience on the part of our friend the goose, she now has something to show for it. The goslings have arrived. May I offer my sincere congratulations!'

'Thank you, thank you, thank you!' said the goose, nodding and bowing shamelessly.

'Thank you,' said the gander.

'Congratulations!' shouted Wilbur. 'How many goslings are there? I can only see one.'

'There are seven,' said the goose.

'Fine!' said Charlotte. 'Seven is a lucky number.'

'Luck had nothing to do with this,' said the goose. 'It was good management and hard work.'

At this point, Templeton showed his nose from his hiding-place under Wilbur's trough. He glanced at Fern, then crept cautiously towards the goose, keeping close to the wall. Everyone watched him, for he was not well liked, not trusted.

'Look,' he began in his sharp voice, 'you say

you have seven goslings. There were eight eggs. What happened to the other egg? Why didn't it hatch?'

'It's a dud, I guess,' said the goose.

'What are you going to do with it?' continued Templeton, his little round beady eyes fixed on the goose.

'You can have it,' replied the goose. 'Roll it away and add it to that nasty collection of yours.' (Templeton had a habit of picking up unusual objects round the farm and storing them in his home. He saved everything.)

'Certainly-ertainly-ertainly,' said the gander. 'You may have the egg. But I'll tell you one thing, Templeton, if I ever catch you poking-oking-oking your ugly nose around our goslings, I'll give you the worst pounding a rat ever took.' And the gander opened his strong wings and beat the air with them to show his power. He was strong and brave, but, the truth is, both the goose and the gander were worried about Templeton. And with good reason. The rat had no morals, no conscience, no scruples, no consideration, no decency, no milk of rodent kindness, no compunctions, no higher feeling, no friendliness, no anything. He would kill a gosling if he could get away with it – the goose knew that. Everybody knew it.

With her broad bill the goose pushed the unhatched egg out of the nest, and the entire company watched in disgust while the rat rolled it away. Even Wilbur, who could eat almost anything, was appalled. 'Imagine wanting a junky old rotten egg!' he muttered.

'A rat is a rat,' said Charlotte. She laughed a tinkling little laugh. 'But, my friends, if that ancient egg ever breaks, this barn will be untenable.'

'What's that mean?' asked Wilbur.

'It means nobody will be able to live here on account of the smell. A rotten egg is a regular stink bomb.'

'I won't break it,' snarled Templeton. 'I know what I'm doing. I handle stuff like this all the time.'

He disappeared into his tunnel, pushing the goose egg in front of him. He pushed and nudged till he succeeded in rolling it to his lair under the trough.

That afternoon, when the wind had died down and the barnyard was quiet and warm, the grey goose led her seven goslings off the nest and out into the world. Mr Zuckerman spied them when he came with Wilbur's supper.

'Well, hello there!' he said, smiling all over. 'Let's see . . . one, two, three, four, five, six, seven. Seven baby geese. Now isn't that lovely!'

Chapter Seven
Bad News

Wilbur liked Charlotte better and better each day. Her campaign against insects seemed sensible and useful. Hardly anybody around the farm had a good word to say for a fly. Flies spent their time pestering others. The cows hated them. The horses detested them. The sheep loathed them. Mr and Mrs Zuckerman were always complaining about them, and putting up screens.

Wilbur admired the way Charlotte managed. He was particularly glad that she always put her victim to sleep before eating it.

'It's real thoughtful of you to do that, Charlotte,' he said.

'Yes,' she replied in her sweet, musical voice, 'I always give them an anaesthetic so they won't feel pain. It's a little service I throw in.'

As the days went by, Wilbur grew and grew. He ate three big meals a day. He spent long hours lying on his side, half asleep, dreaming pleasant dreams. He enjoyed good health and he gained a lot of weight. One afternoon, when Fern was sitting on her stool, the oldest sheep walked into the barn, and stopped to pay a call on Wilbur.

'Hello!' she said. 'Seems to me you're putting on weight.'

'Yes, I guess I am,' replied Wilbur. 'At my age it's a good idea to keep gaining.'

'Just the same, I don't envy you,' said the old sheep. 'You know why they're fattening you up, don't you?'

'No,' said Wilbur.

'Well, I don't like to spread bad news,' said the sheep, 'but they're fattening you up because they're going to kill you, that's why.'

'They're going to *what*?' screamed Wilbur. Fern grew rigid on her stool.

'Kill you. Turn you into smoked bacon and ham,' continued the old sheep. 'Almost all young pigs get murdered by the farmer as soon as the real cold weather sets in. There's a regular conspiracy around here to kill you at Christmastime. Everybody is in the plot – Lurvy, Zuckerman, even John Arable.'

'Mr Arable?' sobbed Wilbur. 'Fern's father?'

'Certainly. When a pig is to be butchered, everybody helps. I'm an old sheep and I see the same thing, same old business, year after year. Arable arrives with his .22, shoots the . . .'

'Stop!' screamed Wilbur. 'I don't want to die! Save me, somebody! Save me!' Fern was just about to jump up when a voice was heard.

'Be quiet, Wilbur!' said Charlotte, who had been listening to this awful conversation.

'I can't be quiet,' screamed Wilbur, racing up

and down. 'I don't want to be killed. I don't want to die. Is it true what the old sheep says, Charlotte? Is it true they are going to kill me when the cold weather comes?'

'Well,' said the spider, plucking thoughtfully at her web, 'the old sheep has been around this barn a long time. She has seen many a spring

pig come and go. If she says they plan to kill you, I'm sure it's true. It's also the dirtiest trick

I ever heard of. What people don't think of!'

Wilbur burst into tears. 'I don't want to die,' he moaned. 'I want to stay alive, right here in my comfortable manure pile with all my friends. I want to breathe the beautiful air and lie in the beautiful sun.'

'You're certainly making a beautiful noise,' snapped the old sheep.

'I don't *want* to die!' screamed Wilbur, throwing himself to the ground.

'You shall not die,' said Charlotte, briskly.

'What? Really?' cried Wilbur. 'Who's going to save me?'

'I am,' said Charlotte.

'How?' asked Wilbur.

'That remains to be seen. But I am going to save you, and I want you to quiet down immediately. You're carrying on in a childish way. Stop your crying! I can't stand hysterics.'

Chapter Eight
A Talk at Home

On Sunday morning Mr and Mrs Arable and Fern were sitting at breakfast in the kitchen. Avery had finished and was upstairs looking for his sling shot.

'Did you know that Uncle Homer's goslings had hatched?' asked Fern.

'How many?' asked Mr Arable.

'Seven,' replied Fern. 'There were eight eggs but one egg didn't hatch and the goose told Templeton she didn't want it any more, so he took it away.'

'The goose did what?' asked Mrs Arable, gazing at her daughter with a queer, worried look.

'Told Templeton she didn't want the egg any

more,' repeated Fern.

'Who is Templeton?' asked Mrs Arable.

'He's the rat,' replied Fern. 'None of us like him much.'

'Who's "us"?' asked Mr Arable.

'Oh, everybody in the barn cellar. Wilbur and the sheep and the lambs and the goose and the gander and the goslings and Charlotte and me.'

'Charlotte?' said Mrs Arable. 'Who's Charlotte?'

'She's Wilbur's best friend. She's terribly clever.'

'What does she look like?' asked Mrs Arable.

'Well-l,' said Fern, thoughtfully, 'she has eight legs. All spiders do, I guess.'

'Charlotte is a spider?' asked Fern's mother.

Fern nodded. 'A big grey one. She has a web across the top of Wilbur's doorway. She catches flies and sucks their blood. Wilbur adores her.'

'Does he really?' said Mrs Arable, rather vaguely. She was staring at Fern with a worried expression on her face.

'Oh, yes, Wilbur adores Charlotte,' said Fern. 'Do you know what Charlotte said when the goslings hatched?'

'I haven't the faintest idea,' said Mr Arable. 'Tell us.'

'Well, when the first gosling stuck its little head out from under the goose, I was sitting on my stool in the corner and Charlotte was on her web. She made a speech. She said: "I am sure that every one of us here in the barn cellar will be gratified to learn that after four weeks of unremitting effort and patience on the part of the goose, she now has something to show for it." Don't you think that was a pleasant thing for her to say?'

'Yes, I do,' said Mrs Arable. 'And now, Fern, it's time to get ready for Sunday School. And tell Avery to get ready. And this afternoon you can tell me more about what goes on in Uncle Homer's barn. Aren't you spending quite a lot of time there? You go there almost every afternoon, don't you?'

'I like it there,' replied Fern. She wiped her mouth and ran upstairs. After she had left the room, Mrs Arable spoke in a low voice to her husband.

'I worry about Fern,' she said. 'Did you hear the way she rambled on about the animals, pretending that they talked?'

Mr Arable chuckled. 'Maybe they do talk,' he said. 'I've sometimes wondered. At any rate, don't worry about Fern – she's just got a lively imagination. Kids think they hear all sorts of things.'

'Just the same, I *do* worry about her,' replied Mrs Arable. 'I think I shall ask Dr Dorian about her the next time I see him. He loves Fern almost as much as we do, and I want him to know how queerly she is acting about that pig and everything. I don't think it's normal. You know perfectly well animals don't talk.'

Mr Arable grinned. 'Maybe our ears aren't as sharp as Fern's,' he said.

Chapter Nine
Wilbur's Boast

A spider's web is stronger than it looks. Although it is made of thin, delicate strands, the web is not easily broken. However, a web gets torn every day by the insects that kick around in it, and a spider must rebuild it when it gets full of holes. Charlotte liked to do her weaving during the late afternoon, and Fern liked to sit near by and watch. One afternoon she heard a most interesting conversation and witnessed a strange event.

'You have awfully hairy legs, Charlotte,' said Wilbur, as the spider busily worked at her task.

'My legs are hairy for a good reason,' replied Charlotte. 'Furthermore, each leg of mine has seven sections – the coxa, the trochanter, the femur, the patella, the tibia, the metatarsus, and the tarsus.'

Wilbur sat bolt upright. 'You're kidding,' he said.

'No, I'm not, either.'

'Say those names again, I didn't catch them the first time.'

'Coxa, trochanter, femur, patella, tibia, metatarsus, and tarsus.'

'Goodness!' said Wilbur, looking down at his own chubby legs. 'I don't think *my* legs have seven sections.'

'Well,' said Charlotte, 'you and I lead different lives. You don't have to spin a web. That takes real leg-work.'

'I could spin a web if I tried,' said Wilbur, boasting. 'I've just never tried.'

'Let's see you do it,' said Charlotte. Fern chuckled softly, and her eyes grew wide with love for the pig.

'OK,' replied Wilbur. 'You coach me and I'll spin one. It must be a lot of fun to spin a web. How do I start?'

'Take a deep breath!' said Charlotte, smiling. Wilbur breathed deeply. 'Now climb to the highest place you can get to, like this.' Charlotte raced up to the top of the doorway. Wilbur scrambled to the top of the manure pile.

'Very good!' said Charlotte. 'Now make an attachment with your spinnerets, hurl yourself into space, and let out a dragline as you go down!'

Wilbur hesitated a moment, then jumped out into the air. He glanced hastily behind to see if a piece of rope was following him to check his fall, but nothing seemed to be happening in his rear, and the next thing he knew he landed with a thump. 'Ooomp!' he grunted.

Charlotte laughed so hard her web began to sway.

'What did I do wrong?' asked the pig, when

he recovered from his bump.

'Nothing,' said Charlotte. 'It was a nice try.'

'I think I'll try again,' said Wilbur, cheerfully. 'I believe what I need is a little piece of string to hold me.'

The pig walked out to his yard. 'You there, Templeton?' he called. The rat poked his head out from under the trough.

'Got a little piece of string I could borrow?' asked Wilbur. 'I need it to spin a web.'

'Yes, indeed,' replied Templeton, who saved string. 'No trouble at all. Anything to oblige.' He crept down into his hole, pushed the goose egg out of the way, and returned with an old piece of dirty white string. Wilbur examined it.

'That's just the thing,' he said. 'Tie one end to my tail, will you, Templeton?'

Wilbur crouched low, with his thin, curly tail towards the rat. Templeton seized the string, passed it round the end of the pig's tail, and tied two half hitches. Charlotte watched in delight.

Like Fern, she was truly fond of Wilbur, whose smelly pen and stale food attracted the flies that she needed, and she was proud to see that he was not a quitter and was willing to try again to spin a web.

While the rat and the spider and the little girl watched, Wilbur climbed again to the top of the manure pile, full of energy and hope.

'Everybody watch!' he cried. And summoning all his strength, he threw himself into the air, head-first. The string trailed behind him. But as he had neglected to fasten the other end to anything, it didn't really do any good, and Wilbur landed with a thud, crushed and hurt. Tears came to his eyes. Templeton grinned. Charlotte just sat quietly. After a bit she spoke.

'You can't spin a web, Wilbur, and I advise you to put the idea out of your mind. You lack two things needed for spinning a web.'

'What are they?' asked Wilbur, sadly.

'You lack a set of spinnerets, and you lack

know-how. But cheer up, you don't need a web. Zuckerman supplies you with three big meals a day. Why should you worry about trapping food?'

Wilbur sighed. 'You're ever so much cleverer and brighter than I am, Charlotte. I guess I was just trying to show off. Serves me right.'

Templeton untied his string and took it back to his home. Charlotte returned to her weaving.

'You needn't feel too badly, Wilbur,' she said. 'Not many creatures can spin webs. Even men aren't as good at it as spiders, although they *think* they're pretty good, and they'll *try* anything. Did you ever hear of the Queensborough Bridge?'

Wilbur shook his head. 'Is it a web?'

'Sort of,' replied Charlotte. 'But do you know how long it took men to build it? Eight whole years. My goodness, I would have starved to death waiting that long. I can make a web in a single evening.'

'What do people catch in the Queensborough Bridge – bugs?' asked Wilbur.

'No,' said Charlotte. 'They don't catch anything. They just keep trotting back and forth across the bridge thinking there is something better on the other side. If they'd hang head-down at the top of the thing and wait quietly, maybe something good would come along. But no – with men it's rush, rush, rush, every minute. I'm glad I'm a sedentary spider.'

'What does sedentary mean?' asked Wilbur.

'Means I sit still a good part of the time and don't go wandering all over creation. I know a good thing when I see it, and my web is a good thing. I stay put and wait for what comes. Gives me a chance to think.'

'Well, I'm sort of sedentary myself, I guess,' said the pig. 'I have to hang around here whether I want to or not. You know where I'd really like to be this evening?'

'Where?'

'In a forest looking for beech nuts and truffles and delectable roots, pushing leaves aside with my wonderful strong nose, searching and sniffing along the ground, smelling, smelling, smelling . . .'

'You smell just the way you are,' remarked a lamb who had just walked in. 'I can smell you from here. You're the smelliest creature in the place.'

Wilbur hung his head. His eyes grew wet with tears. Charlotte noticed his embarrassment and she spoke sharply to the lamb.

'Let Wilbur alone!' she said. 'He has a perfect right to smell, considering his surroundings. You're no bundle of sweet peas yourself. Furthermore, you are interrupting a very pleasant conversation. What were we talking about, Wilbur, when we were so rudely interrupted?'

'Oh, I don't remember,' said Wilbur. 'It doesn't make any difference. Let's not talk any more for a while, Charlotte. I'm getting sleepy. You go ahead and finish fixing your web and I'll just lie here and watch you. It's a lovely evening.' Wilbur stretched out on his side and sighed a long sigh.

Twilight settled over Zuckerman's barn, and a feeling of peace. Fern knew it was almost suppertime but she couldn't bear to leave. Swallows passed on silent wings, in and out of the doorways, bringing food to their young ones. From across the road a bird sang 'Whippoorwill, whippoorwill!' Lurvy sat down under an apple tree and lit his pipe: the animals sniffed the familiar smell of strong tobacco. Wilbur heard the trill of the tree toad and the occasional slamming of the kitchen door. All these sounds made him comfortable and happy, for he loved life and loved to be a part of the world on a summer evening. But as he lay there he remembered what the old sheep had told him. The thought of death came to him and he began to tremble with fear.

'Charlotte?' he said, softly.

'Yes, Wilbur?'

'I don't want to die.'

'Of course you don't,' said Charlotte in a comforting voice.

'I just love it here in the barn,' said Wilbur. 'I love everything about this place.'

'Of course you do,' said Charlotte. 'We all do.'

The goose appeared, followed by her seven goslings. They thrust their little necks out and kept up a musical whistling, like a tiny troupe of pipers. Wilbur listened to the sound with love in his heart.

'Charlotte?' he said.

'Yes?' said the spider.

'Were you serious when you promised you would keep them from killing me?'

'I was never more serious in my life. I am not going to let you die, Wilbur.'

'How are you going to save me?' asked Wilbur, whose curiosity was very strong on this point.

'Well,' said Charlotte, vaguely, 'I don't really know. But I'm working on a plan.'

'That's wonderful,' said Wilbur. 'How is the plan coming, Charlotte? Have you got very far with it? Is it coming along pretty well?' Wilbur was trembling again, but Charlotte was cool and collected.

'Oh, it's coming all right,' she said, lightly. 'The plan is still in its early stages and hasn't completely shaped up yet, but I'm working on it.'

'When do you work on it?' begged Wilbur.

'When I'm hanging head-down at the top of my web. That's when I do my thinking, because then all the blood is in my head.'

'I'd be only too glad to help in any way I can.'

'Oh, I'll work it out alone,' said Charlotte. 'I can think better if I think alone.'

'All right,' said Wilbur. 'But don't fail to let me know if there's anything I can do to help, no matter how slight.'

'Well,' replied Charlotte, 'you must try to build yourself up. I want you to get plenty of sleep, and stop worrying. Never hurry and never worry! Chew your food thoroughly and eat every bit of it, except you must leave just enough for Templeton. Gain weight and stay well – that's the way you can help. Keep fit, and don't lose your nerve. Do you think you understand?'

'Yes, I understand,' said Wilbur.

'Go along to bed then,' said Charlotte. 'Sleep is important.'

Wilbur trotted over to the darkest corner of his pen and threw himself down. He closed his eyes. In another minute he spoke.

'Charlotte?' he said.

'Yes, Wilbur?'

'May I go out to my trough and see if I left

any of my supper? I think I left just a tiny bit of mashed potato.'

'Very well,' said Charlotte. 'But I want you in bed again without delay.'

Wilbur started to race out to his yard.

'Slowly, slowly!' said Charlotte. 'Never hurry and never worry!'

Wilbur checked himself and crept slowly to his trough. He found a bit of potato, chewed it carefully, swallowed it, and walked back to bed. He closed his eyes and was silent for a while.

'Charlotte?' he said, in a whisper.

'Yes?'

'May I get a drink of milk? I think there are a few drops of milk left in my trough.'

'No, the trough is dry, and I want you to go to sleep. No more talking! Close your eyes and go to sleep!'

Wilbur shut his eyes. Fern got up from her stool and started for home, her mind full of everything she had seen and heard.

'Good night, Charlotte!' said Wilbur.

'Good night, Wilbur!'

There was a pause.

'Good night, Charlotte!'

'Good night, Wilbur!'

'Good night!'

'Good night!'

Chapter Ten
An Explosion

D ay after day the spider waited, head-
down, for an idea to come to her. Hour by
hour she sat motionless, deep in thought.
Having promised Wilbur that she would save
his life, she was determined to keep her
promise.

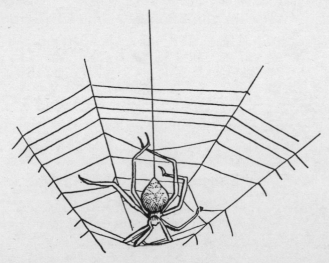

Charlotte was naturally patient. She knew from experience that if she waited long enough, a fly would come to her web; and she felt sure that if she thought long enough about Wilbur's problem, an idea would come to her mind.

Finally, one morning towards the middle of July, the idea came. 'Why, how perfectly simple!' she said to herself. 'The way to save Wilbur's life is to play a trick on Zuckerman. If I can fool a bug,' thought Charlotte, 'I can surely fool a man. People are not as smart as bugs.'

Wilbur walked into his yard just at that moment.

'What are you thinking about, Charlotte?' he asked.

'I was just thinking,' said the spider, 'that people are very gullible.'

'What does "gullible" mean?'

'Easy to fool,' said Charlotte.

'That's a mercy,' replied Wilbur, and he lay down in the shade of his fence and went fast asleep. The spider, however, stayed wide awake, gazing affectionately at him and making plans for his future. Summer was half gone. She knew she didn't have much time.

That morning, just as Wilbur fell asleep, Avery Arable wandered into the Zuckermans' front yard, followed by Fern. Avery carried a live frog in his hand. Fern had a crown of daisies in her hair. The children ran for the kitchen.

'Just in time for a piece of blueberry pie,' said Mrs Zuckerman.

'Look at my frog!' said Avery, placing the frog on the drainboard and holding out his hand for pie.

'Take that thing out of here!' said Mrs Zuckerman.

'He's hot,' said Fern. 'He's almost dead, that frog.'

'He is not,' said Avery. 'He lets me scratch him between the eyes.' The frog jumped and landed in Mrs Zuckerman's dishpan full of soapy water.

'You're getting your pie on you,' said Fern. 'Can I look for eggs in the henhouse, Aunt Edith?'

'Run outdoors, both of you! And don't bother the hens!'

'It's getting all over everything,' shouted Fern. 'His pie is all over his front.'

'Come on, frog!' cried Avery. He scooped up his frog. The frog kicked, splashing soapy water on to the blueberry pie.

'Another crisis!' groaned Fern.

'Let's swing in the swing!' said Avery.

The children ran to the barn.

Mr Zuckerman had the best swing in the county. It was a single long piece of heavy rope tied to the beam over the north doorway. At the bottom end of the rope was a fat knot to sit on. It was arranged so that you could swing without being pushed. You climbed a ladder to the hayloft. Then, holding the rope, you stood at the edge and looked down, and were scared and dizzy. Then you straddled the knot, so that it acted as a seat. Then you got up all your nerve, took a deep breath, and jumped. For a second you seemed to be falling to the barn floor far below, but then suddenly the rope would begin to catch you, and you would sail through the barn door going a mile a minute, with the wind whistling in your eyes and ears and hair. Then you would zoom upwards into the sky, and look up at the clouds, and the rope would twist and you would twist and turn with the rope. Then you would drop down, down, down out of the sky and come sailing back into the barn almost into the hayloft, then sail out again (not quite so far this time), then in again (not quite so high), then out again, then in again, then out, then in; and then you'd jump off and fall down and let somebody else try it.

Mothers for miles around worried about

Zuckerman's swing. They feared some child would fall off. But no child ever did. Children almost always hang on to things tighter than their parents think they will.

Avery put the frog in his pocket and climbed to the hay loft. 'The last time I swang in this swing, I almost crashed into a barn swallow,' he yelled.

'Take that frog out!' ordered Fern.

Avery straddled the rope and jumped. He sailed out through the door, frog and all, and into the sky, frog and all. Then he sailed back into the barn.

'Your tongue is purple!' screamed Fern.

'So is yours!' cried Avery, sailing out again with the frog.

'I have hay inside my dress! It itches!' called Fern.

'Scratch it!' yelled Avery, as he sailed back.

'It's my turn,' said Fern. 'Jump off!'

'Fern's got the itch!' sang Avery.

When he jumped off, he threw the swing up to his sister. She shut her eyes tight and jumped. She felt the dizzy drop, then the supporting lift of the swing. When she opened her eyes she was looking up into the blue sky and was about to fly back through the door.

They took turns for an hour.

When the children grew tired of swinging, they went down towards the pasture and picked wild raspberries and ate them. Their tongues turned from purple to red. Fern bit into a raspberry that had a bad-tasting bug inside it, and got discouraged. Avery found an empty candy box and put his frog in it. The frog seemed tired after his morning in the swing. The children walked slowly up towards the barn. They, too, were tired and hardly had energy enough to walk.

'Let's build a tree house,' suggested Avery. 'I want to live in a tree, with my frog.'

'I'm going to visit Wilbur,' Fern announced.

They climbed the fence into the lane and walked lazily towards the pigpen. Wilbur heard them coming and got up.

Avery noticed the spider web, and, coming closer, he saw Charlotte.

'Hey, look at that big spider!' he said. 'It's tremenjus.'

'Leave it alone!' commanded Fern. 'You've got a frog – isn't that enough?'

'That's a fine spider and I'm going to capture it,' said Avery. He took the cover off the candy box. Then he picked up a stick. 'I'm going to knock that ol' spider into this box,' he said.

Wilbur's heart almost stopped when he saw what was going on. This might be the end of Charlotte if the boy succeeded in catching her.

'You stop it, Avery!' cried Fern.

Avery put one leg over the fence of the pigpen. He was just about to raise his stick to hit Charlotte when he lost his balance. He swayed and toppled and landed on the edge of Wilbur's trough. The trough tipped up and then came down with a slap. The goose egg was right underneath. There was a dull explosion as the egg broke, and then a horrible smell.

Fern screamed. Avery jumped to his feet. The air was filled with the terrible gases and smells from the rotten egg. Templeton, who had been

resting in his home, scuttled away into the barn.

'Good *night*!' screamed Avery. 'Good *night*! What a stink! Let's get out of here!'

Fern was crying. She held her nose and ran towards the house. Avery ran after her, holding his nose. Charlotte felt greatly relieved to see him go. It had been a narrow escape.

Later on that morning, the animals came up from the pasture – the sheep, the lambs, the gander, the goose, and the seven goslings. There were many complaints about the awful smell, and Wilbur had to tell the story over and over again, of how the Arable boy had tried to capture Charlotte, and how the smell of the broken egg drove him away just in time. 'It was that rotten goose egg that saved Charlotte's life,' said Wilbur.

The goose was proud of her share in the adventure. 'I'm delighted that the egg never hatched,' she gabbled.

Templeton, of course, was miserable over the loss of his beloved egg. But he couldn't resist boasting. 'It pays to save things,' he said in his surly voice. 'A rat never knows when something is going to come in handy. I never throw anything away.'

'Well,' said one of the lambs, 'this whole business is all well and good for Charlotte, but what about the rest of us? The smell is unbearable. Who wants to live in a barn that is perfumed with rotten egg?'

'Don't worry, you'll get used to it,' said Templeton. He sat up and pulled wisely at his long whiskers, then crept away to pay a visit to the dump.

When Lurvy showed up at lunchtime carrying a pail of food for Wilbur, he stopped short a few paces from the pigpen. He sniffed the air and made a face.

'What in thunder?' he said. Setting the pail down, he picked up the stick that Avery had dropped and pried the trough up. 'Rats!' he said. 'Phew! I might a' known a rat would make a nest under this trough. How I hate a rat!'

And Lurvy dragged Wilbur's trough across the yard and kicked some dirt into the rat's nest, burying the broken egg and all Templeton's other possessions. Then he picked up the pail. Wilbur stood in the trough, drooling with hunger. Lurvy poured. The slops ran creamily down around the pig's eyes and ears. Wilbur grunted. He gulped and sucked, and sucked and gulped, making swishing and swooshing noises, anxious to get everything at once. It was a delicious meal – skim milk, wheat middlings, left-over pancakes, half a doughnut, the rind of a summer squash, two pieces of stale toast, a third of a ginger snap, a fish tail, one orange peel, several noodles from a noodle soup, the skin off a cup of cocoa, an ancient jelly roll, a strip of paper from the lining of the garbage pail, and a spoonful of raspberry jelly.

Wilbur ate heartily. He planned to leave half a noodle and a few drops of milk for Templeton. Then he remembered that the rat had been useful in saving Charlotte's life, and that Charlotte was trying to save *his* life. So he left a whole noodle, instead of a half.

Now that the broken egg was buried, the air cleared and the barn smelt good again. The afternoon passed, and evening came. Shadows lengthened. The cool and kindly breath of evening entered through doors and windows.

Astride her web, Charlotte sat moodily eating a horse-fly and thinking about the future. After a while she bestirred herself.

She descended to the centre of the web and there she began to cut some of her lines. She worked slowly but steadily while the other creatures drowsed. None of the others, not even the goose, noticed that she was at work. Deep in his soft bed, Wilbur snoozed. Over in their favourite corner, the goslings whistled a night song.

Charlotte tore quite a section out of her web, leaving an open space in the middle. Then she started weaving something to take the place of the threads she had removed. When Templeton got back from the dump, around midnight, the spider was still at work.

Chapter Eleven
The Miracle

The next day was foggy. Everything on the farm was dripping wet. The grass looked like a magic carpet. The asparagus patch looked like a silver forest.

On foggy mornings, Charlotte's web was truly a thing of beauty. This morning each thin strand was decorated with dozens of tiny beads of water. The web glistened in the light and made a pattern of loveliness and mystery, like a delicate veil. Even Lurvy, who wasn't particularly interested in beauty, noticed the web when he came with the pig's breakfast. He noted how clearly it showed up and he noted how big and carefully built it was. And then he took another look and he saw something that made him set his pail down. There, in the centre of the web, neatly woven in block letters, was a message. It said:

SOME PIG

Lurvy felt weak. He brushed his hand across his eyes and stared harder at Charlotte's web.

'I'm seeing things,' he whispered. He dropped to his knees and uttered a short prayer. Then, forgetting all about Wilbur's breakfast, he walked back to the house and called Mr Zuckerman.

'I think you'd better come down to the pigpen,' he said.

'What's the trouble?' asked Mr Zuckerman. 'Anything wrong with the pig?'

'No – not exactly,' said Lurvy. 'Come and see for yourself.'

The two men walked silently down to Wilbur's yard. Lurvy pointed to the spider's web. 'Do you see what I see?' he asked.

Zuckerman stared at the writing on the web. Then he murmured the words 'Some pig'. Then he looked at Lurvy. Then they both began to tremble. Charlotte, sleepy after her night's exertions, smiled as she watched. Wilbur came and stood directly under the web.

'Some pig!' muttered Lurvy in a low voice.

'Some pig!' whispered Mr Zuckerman. They stared and stared for a long time at Wilbur. Then they stared at Charlotte.

'You don't suppose that that spider . . .' began Mr Zuckerman – but he shook his head and didn't finish the sentence. Instead, he walked solemnly back up to the house and spoke to his wife. 'Edith, something has happened,' he said, in a weak voice. He went into the living-room and sat down, and Mrs Zuckerman followed.

'I've got something to tell you, Edith,' he said. 'You better sit down.'

Mrs Zuckerman sank into a chair. She looked pale and frightened.

'Edith,' he said, trying to keep his voice steady, 'I think you had best be told that we have a very unusual pig.'

A look of complete bewilderment came over Mrs Zuckerman's face. 'Homer Zuckerman, what in the world are you talking about?' she said.

'This is a very serious thing, Edith,' he replied. 'Our pig is completely out of the ordinary.'

'What's unusual about the pig?' asked Mrs Zuckerman, who was beginning to recover from her scare.

'Well, I don't really know yet,' said Mr
Zuckerman. 'But we have received a sign, Edith
– a mysterious sign. A miracle has happened on
this farm. There is a large spider's web in the
doorway of the barn cellar, right over the
pigpen, and when Lurvy went to feed the pig
this morning, he noticed the web because it was
foggy, and you know how a spider's web looks
very distinct in a fog. And right spang in the
middle of the web there were the words "Some
pig". The words were woven right into the web.
They were actually part of the web, Edith. I
know, because I have been down there and seen
them. It says, "Some pig", just as clear as clear
can be. There can be no mistake about it. A
miracle has happened and a sign has occurred
here on earth, right on our farm, and we have
no ordinary pig.'

'Well,' said Mrs Zuckerman, 'it seems to me
you're a little off. It seems to me we have no
ordinary *spider*.'

'Oh, no,' said Zuckerman. 'It's the pig that's unusual. It says so, right there in the middle of the web.'

'Maybe so,' said Mrs Zuckerman. 'Just the same, I intend to have a look at that spider.'

'It's just a common grey spider,' said Zuckerman.

They got up, and together they walked down to Wilbur's yard. 'You see, Edith? It's just a common grey spider.'

Wilbur was pleased to receive so much attention. Lurvy was still standing there, and Mr and Mrs Zuckerman, all three, stood for about an hour, reading the words on the web over and over, and watching Wilbur.

Charlotte was delighted with the way her trick was working. She sat without moving a muscle, and listened to the conversation of the people. When a small fly blundered into the web, just beyond the word 'pig', Charlotte dropped quickly down, rolled the fly up, and carried it out of the way.

After a while the fog lifted. The web dried off and the words didn't show up so plainly. The Zuckermans and Lurvy walked back to the house. Just before they left the pigpen, Mr Zuckerman took one last look at Wilbur.

'You know,' he said, in an important voice, 'I've thought all along that that pig of ours was an extra good one. He's a solid pig. That pig is as solid as they come. You notice how solid he is around the shoulders, Lurvy?'

'Sure, sure I do,' said Lurvy. 'I've always noticed that pig. He's quite a pig.'

'He's long, and he's smooth,' said Zuckerman.

'That's right,' agreed Lurvy. 'He's as smooth as they come. He's some pig.'

When Mr Zuckerman got back to the house, he took off his work clothes and put on his best suit. Then he got into his car and drove to the minister's house. He stayed for an hour and explained to the minister that a miracle had happened on the farm.

'So far,' said Zuckerman, 'only four people on earth know about this miracle – myself, my wife Edith, my hired man Lurvy, and you.'

'Don't tell anybody else,' said the minister. 'We don't know what it means yet, but perhaps if I give thought to it, I can explain it in my sermon next Sunday. There can be no doubt that you have a most unusual pig. I intend to speak about it in my sermon and point out the fact that this community has been visited with a

wondrous animal. By the way, does the pig have a name?'

'Why, yes,' said Mr Zuckerman. 'My little niece calls him Wilbur. She's a rather queer child – full of notions. She raised the pig on a bottle and I bought him from her when he was a month old.'

He shook hands with the minister, and left.

Secrets are hard to keep. Long before Sunday came, the news spread all over the county. Everybody knew that a sign had appeared in a spider's web on the Zuckerman place. Everybody knew that the Zuckermans had a wondrous pig. People came from miles around to look at Wilbur and to read the words on Charlotte's web. The Zuckermans' driveway was full of cars and trucks from morning till night – Fords and Chevvies and Buick roadmasters and GMC pickups and Plymouths and Studebakers and Packards and De Sotos with gyromatic transmissions and Oldsmobiles with rocket engines and Jeep station wagons and Pontiacs. The news of the wonderful pig spread clear up into the hills, and farmers came rattling down in buggies and buckboards, to stand hour after hour at Wilbur's pen admiring the miraculous animal. All said they had never seen such a pig before in their lives.

When Fern told her mother that Avery had tried to hit the Zuckermans' spider with a stick, Mrs Arable was so shocked that she sent Avery to bed without any supper, as punishment.

In the days that followed, Mr Zuckerman was so busy entertaining visitors that he neglected his farm work. He wore his good clothes all the time now – got right into them when he got up in the morning. Mrs Zuckerman prepared special meals for Wilbur. Lurvy shaved and got a haircut; and his principal farm duty was to feed the pig while people looked on.

Mr Zuckerman ordered Lurvy to increase

Wilbur's feedings from three meals a day to four meals a day. The Zuckermans were so busy with visitors they forgot about other things on the farm. The blackberries got ripe, and Mrs Zuckerman never put up any blackberry jam. The corn needed hoeing and Lurvy didn't find time to hoe it.

On Sunday the church was full. The minister explained the miracle. He said that the words on the spider's web proved that human beings must always be on the watch for the coming of wonders.

All in all, the Zuckermans' pigpen was the centre of attraction. Fern was happy, for she felt that Charlotte's trick was working and that Wilbur's life would be saved. But she found that the barn was not nearly so pleasant – too many people. She liked it better when she could be all alone with her friends the animals.

Chapter Twelve
A Meeting

One evening, a few days after the writing had appeared in Charlotte's web, the spider called a meeting of all the animals in the barn cellar.

'I shall begin by calling the roll. Wilbur?'

'Here!' said the pig.

'Gander?'

'Here, here, here!' said the gander.

'You sound like three ganders,' muttered Charlotte. 'Why can't you just say "here"? Why do you have to repeat everything?'

'It's my idio-idio-idiosyncrasy,' replied the gander.

'Goose?' said Charlotte.

'Here, here, here!' said the goose. Charlotte glared at her.

'Goslings, one through seven?'

'Bee-bee-bee!' Bee-bee-bee!' 'Bee-bee-bee!' 'Bee-bee-bee!' 'Bee-bee-bee!' 'Bee-bee-bee!' 'Bee-bee-bee!' said the goslings.

'This is getting to be quite a meeting,' said Charlotte. 'Anybody would think we had three ganders, three geese, and twenty-one goslings. Sheep?'

'He-aa-aa!' answered the sheep all together.

'Lambs?'

'He-aa-aa!' answered the lambs all together.

'Templeton?'

No answer.

'Templeton?'

No answer.

'Well, we are all here except the rat,' said Charlotte. 'I guess we can proceed without him. Now, all of you must have noticed what's been going on around here the last few days. The message I wrote in my web, praising Wilbur, has been received. The Zuckermans have fallen for it, and so has everybody else. Zuckerman thinks Wilbur is an unusual pig, and therefore he won't want to kill him and eat him. I dare say my trick will work and Wilbur's life can be saved.'

'Hurray!' cried everybody.

'Thank you very much,' said Charlotte. 'Now I called this meeting in order to get suggestions. I need new ideas for the web. People are already getting sick of reading the words "SOME PIG". If anybody can think of another message, or remark, I'll be glad to weave it into the web. Any suggestions for a new slogan?'

'How about "Pig Supreme"?' asked one of the lambs.

'No good,' said Charlotte. 'It sounds like a rich dessert.'

'How about "Terrific, terrific, terrific"?' asked the goose.

'Cut that down to one "terrific" and it will do very nicely,' said Charlotte. 'I think "terrific" might impress Zuckerman.'

'But, Charlotte,' said Wilbur, 'I'm not terrific.'

'That doesn't make a particle of difference,'

replied Charlotte. 'Not a particle. People believe almost anything they see in print. Does anybody here know how to spell "terrific"?'

'I think,' said the gander, 'it's tee double ee double rr double rr double eye double ff double eye double see see see see see.'

'What kind of an acrobat do you think I am?' said Charlotte in disgust. 'I would have to have St Vitus's Dance to weave a word like that into my web.'

'Sorry, sorry, sorry,' said the gander.

Then the oldest sheep spoke up. 'I agree that there should be something new written in the web if Wilbur's life is to be saved. And if Charlotte needs help in finding words, I think she can get it from our friend Templeton. The rat visits the dump regularly and has access to old magazines. He can tear out bits of advertisements and bring them up here to the barn cellar, so that Charlotte can have something to copy.'

'Good idea,' said Charlotte. 'But I'm not sure Templeton will be willing to help. You know how he is – always looking out for himself, never thinking of the other fellow.'

'I bet I can get him to help,' said the old sheep. 'I'll appeal to his baser instincts, of which he has plenty. Here he comes now. Everybody keep quiet while I put the matter up to him!'

The rat entered the barn the way he always did – creeping along close to the wall.

'What's up?' he asked, seeing the animals assembled.

'We're holding a directors' meeting,' replied the old sheep.

'Well, break it up!' said Templeton. 'Meetings bore me.' And the rat began to climb a rope that hung against the wall.

'Look,' said the old sheep, 'next time you go to the dump, Templeton, bring back a clipping from a magazine. Charlotte needs new ideas so she can write messages in her web and save Wilbur's life.'

'Let him die,' said the rat. 'I should worry.'

'You'll worry all right when next winter comes,' said the sheep. 'You'll worry all right on a zero morning next January when Wilbur is dead and nobody comes down here with a nice pail of warm slops to pour into the trough. Wilbur's left-over food is your chief source of supply, Templeton. *You* know that. Wilbur's food is your food; therefore Wilbur's destiny and your destiny are closely linked. If Wilbur is killed and his trough stands empty day after day, you'll grow so thin we can look right through your stomach and see objects on the other side.'

Templeton's whiskers quivered.

'Maybe you're right,' he said gruffly. 'I'm making a trip to the dump tomorrow afternoon. I'll bring back a magazine clipping if I can find one.'

'Thanks,' said Charlotte. 'The meeting is now adjourned. I have a busy evening ahead of me. I've got to tear my web apart and write TERRIFIC.'

Wilbur blushed. 'But I'm *not* terrific, Charlotte. I'm just about average for a pig.'

'You're terrific as far as *I'm* concerned,' replied Charlotte, sweetly, 'and that's what counts. You're my best friend, and *I* think you're sensational. Now stop arguing and go get some sleep!'

Chapter Thirteen
Good Progress

F ar into the night, while the other creatures slept, Charlotte worked on her web. First she ripped out a few of the orb lines near the centre. She left the radial lines alone, as they were needed for support. As she worked, her eight legs were a great help to her. So were her teeth. She loved to weave and she was an expert at it. When she had finished ripping things out, her web looked something like this:

A spider can produce several kinds of thread. She uses a dry, tough thread for foundation lines, and she uses a sticky thread for snare lines – the ones that catch and hold insects. Charlotte decided to use her dry thread for writing the new message.

'If I write the word TERRIFIC with sticky thread,' she thought, 'every bug that comes along will get stuck in it and spoil the effect.'

'Now let's see, the first letter is T.'

Charlotte climbed to a point at the top of the left-hand side of the web. Swinging her spinnerets into position, she attached her thread and then dropped down. As she dropped, her spinning tubes went into action and she let out thread. At the bottom, she attached the thread. This formed the upright part of the letter T. Charlotte was not satisfied, however. She climbed up and made another attachment, right next to the first. Then she carried the line down, so that she had a double line instead of a single line. 'It will show up better if I make the whole thing with double lines.'

She climbed back up, moved over about an inch to the left, touched her spinnerets to the web, and then carried a line across to the right, forming the top of the T. She repeated this, making it double. Her eight legs were very busy helping.

'Now for the E!'

Charlotte got so interested in her work, she began to talk to herself, as though to cheer herself on. If you had been sitting quietly in the barn cellar that evening, you would have heard something like this:

'Now for the R! Up we go! Attach! Descend! Pay out line! Whoa! Attach! Good! Up you go! Repeat! Attach! Descend! Pay out line. Whoa, girl! Steady now! Attach! Climb! Attach! Over to the right! Pay out line! Attach! Now right and down and swing that loop and around and around! Now in to the left! Attach! Climb!

Repeat! OK! Easy, keep those lines together! Now, then, out and down for the leg of the R! Pay out line! Whoa! Attach! Ascend! Repeat! Good girl!'

And so, talking to herself, the spider worked at her difficult task. When it was completed, she felt hungry. She ate a small bug that she had been saving. Then she slept.

Next morning, Wilbur arose and stood beneath the web. He breathed the morning air into his lungs. Drops of dew, catching the sun, made the web stand out clearly. When Lurvy arrived with breakfast, there was the handsome pig, and over him, woven neatly in block letters, was the word TERRIFIC. Another miracle.

Lurvy rushed and called Mr Zuckerman. Mr Zuckerman rushed and called Mrs Zuckerman. Mrs Zuckerman ran to the phone and called the Arables. The Arables climbed into their truck and hurried over. Everybody stood at the pigpen and stared at the web and read the

word, over and over, while Wilbur, who really
felt terrific, stood quietly swelling out his chest
and swinging his snout from side to side.

'Terrific!' breathed Zuckerman, in joyful admiration. 'Edith, you better phone the reporter on the *Weekly Chronicle* and tell him what has happened. He will want to know about this. He may want to bring a photographer. There isn't a pig in the whole state that is as terrific as our pig.'

The news spread. People who had journeyed to see Wilbur when he was 'some pig' came back again to see him now that he was 'terrific'.

That afternoon, when Mr Zuckerman went to milk the cows and clean out the tie-ups, he was still thinking about what a wondrous pig he owned.

'Lurvy!' he called. 'There is to be no more cow manure thrown down into that pigpen. I have a terrific pig. I want that pig to have clean, bright straw every day for his bedding. Understand?'

'Yes, sir,' said Lurvy.

'Furthermore,' said Mr Zuckerman, 'I want

you to start building a crate for Wilbur. I have decided to take the pig to the County Fair on September sixth. Make the crate large and paint it green with gold letters!'

'What will the letters say?' asked Lurvy.

'They should say *Zuckerman's Famous Pig.*'

Lurvy picked up a pitchfork and walked away to get some clean straw. Having such an important pig was going to mean plenty of extra work, he could see that.

Below the apple orchard, at the end of the path, was the dump where Mr Zuckerman threw all sorts of trash and stuff that nobody wanted any more. Here, in a small clearing hidden by young alders and wild raspberry bushes, was an astonishing pile of old bottles and empty tin cans and dirty rags and bits of metal and broken bottles and broken hinges and broken springs and dead batteries and last month's magazines and old discarded dishmops and tattered overalls and rusty spikes and leaky pails and forgotten stoppers and useless junk of all kinds, including a wrong-size crank for a broken ice-cream freezer.

Templeton knew the dump and liked it. There were good hiding-places there – excellent cover for a rat. And there was usually a tin can with food still clinging to the inside.

Templeton was down there now, rummaging around. When he returned to the barn, he carried in his mouth an advertisement he had torn from a crumpled magazine.

'How's this?' he asked, showing the ad. to Charlotte. 'It says CRUNCHY. "Crunchy" would be a good word to write in your web.'

'Just the wrong idea,' replied Charlotte. 'Couldn't be worse. We don't want Zuckerman to think Wilbur is crunchy. He might start thinking about crisp, crunchy bacon and tasty ham. That would put ideas into his head. We must advertise Wilbur's noble qualities, not his tastiness. Go get another word, please, Templeton!'

The rat looked disgusted. But he sneaked away to the dump and was back in a while with a strip of cotton cloth. 'How's this?' he asked. 'It's a label off an old shirt.'

Charlotte examined the label. It said PRESHRUNK.

'I'm sorry, Templeton,' she said, 'but PRESHRUNK is out of the question. We want Zuckerman to think Wilbur is nicely filled out, not all shrunk up. I'll have to ask you to try again.'

'What do you think I am, a messenger boy?'

grumbled the rat. 'I'm not going to spend all my time chasing down to the dump after advertising material.'

'Just once more – please!' said Charlotte.

'I'll tell you what I'll do,' said Templeton. 'I know where there's a package of soap flakes in the woodshed. It has writing on it. I'll bring you a piece of the package.'

He climbed the rope that hung on the wall and disappeared through a hole in the ceiling. When he came back he had a strip of blue-and-white cardboard in his teeth.

'There!' he said, triumphantly. 'How's that?'

Charlotte read the words: 'With New Radiant Action.'

'What does it mean?' asked Charlotte, who had never used any soap flakes in her life.

'How should I know?' said Templeton. 'You asked for words and I brought them. I suppose the next thing you'll want me to fetch is a dictionary.'

Together they studied the soap ad. 'With new radiant action,' repeated Charlotte, slowly. 'Wilbur!' she called.

Wilbur, who was asleep in the straw, jumped up.

'Run around!' commanded Charlotte. 'I want to see you in action, to see if you are radiant.'

Wilbur raced to the end of his yard.

'Now back again, faster!' said Charlotte.

Wilbur galloped back. His skin shone. His tail had a fine, tight curl in it.

'Jump into the air!' cried Charlotte.

Wilbur jumped as high as he could.

'Keep your knees straight and touch the ground with your ears!' called Charlotte.

Wilbur obeyed.

'Do a back flip with a half twist in it!' cried Charlotte.

Wilbur went over backwards, writhing and twisting as he went.

'OK, Wilbur,' said Charlotte. 'You can go

back to sleep. OK, Templeton, the soap ad. will do, I guess. I'm not sure Wilbur's action is exactly radiant, but it's interesting.'

'Actually,' said Wilbur, 'I *feel* radiant.'

'Do you?' said Charlotte, looking at him with affection. 'Well, you're a good little pig, and radiant you shall be. I'm in this thing pretty deep now – I might as well go the limit.'

Tired from his romp, Wilbur lay down in the clean straw. He closed his eyes. The straw seemed scratchy – not as comfortable as the cow manure, which was always delightfully soft to lie in. So he pushed the straw to one side and stretched out in the manure. Wilbur sighed. It had been a busy day – his first day of being terrific. Dozens of people had visited his yard during the afternoon, and he had had to stand and pose, looking as terrific as he could. Now he was tired. Fern had arrived and seated herself quietly on her stool in the corner.

'Tell me a story, Charlotte!' said Wilbur, as he

lay waiting for sleep to come. 'Tell me a story!'

So Charlotte, although she, too, was tired, did what Wilbur wanted.

'Once upon a time,' she began, 'I had a beautiful cousin who managed to build her web across a small stream. One day a tiny fish leaped into the air and got tangled in the web. My cousin was very much surprised, of course. The fish was thrashing wildly. My cousin hardly dared tackle it. But she did. She swooped

down and threw great masses of wrapping material around the fish and fought bravely to capture it.'

'Did she succeed?' asked Wilbur.

'It was a never-to-be-forgotten battle,' said Charlotte. 'There was the fish, caught only by one fin, and its tail wildly thrashing and shining in the sun. There was the web, sagging dangerously under the weight of the fish.'

'How much did the fish weigh?' asked Wilbur eagerly.

'I don't know,' said Charlotte. 'There was my

cousin, slipping in, dodging out, beaten mercilessly over the head by the wildly thrashing fish, dancing in, dancing out, throwing her threads and fighting hard. First she threw a left around the tail. The fish lashed back. Then a left to the tail and a right to the mid-section. The fish lashed back. Then she dodged to one side and threw a right, and another right to the fin. Then a hard left to the head, while the web swayed and stretched.'

'Then what happened?' asked Wilbur.

'Nothing,' said Charlotte. 'The fish lost the fight. My cousin wrapped it up so tight it couldn't budge.'

'Then what happened?' asked Wilbur.

'Nothing,' said Charlotte. 'My cousin kept the fish for a while, and then, when she got good and ready, she ate it.'

'Tell me another story!' begged Wilbur.

So Charlotte told him about another cousin of hers who was an aeronaut.

'What is an aeronaut?' asked Wilbur.

'A balloonist,' said Charlotte. 'My cousin used to stand on her head and let out enough thread to form a balloon. Then she'd let go and be lifted into the air and carried upwards on the warm wind.'

'Is that true?' asked Wilbur. 'Or are you just making it up?'

'It's true,' replied Charlotte. 'I have some very remarkable cousins. And now, Wilbur, it's time you went to sleep.'

'Sing something!' begged Wilbur, closing his eyes.

So Charlotte sang a lullaby, while crickets chirped in the grass and the barn grew dark. This was the song she sang:

> 'Sleep, sleep, my love, my only,
> Deep, deep, in the dung and the dark;
> Be not afraid and be not lonely!
> This is the hour when frogs and thrushes

Praise the world from the woods and the rushes.
Rest from care, my one and only,
Deep in the dung and the dark!'

But Wilbur was already asleep. When the song ended, Fern got up and went home.

Chapter Fourteen
Dr Dorian

The next day was Saturday. Fern stood at the kitchen sink drying the breakfast dishes as her mother washed them. Mrs Arable worked silently. She hoped Fern would go out and play with other children, instead of heading for the Zuckermans' barn to sit and watch animals.

'Charlotte is the best storyteller I ever heard,' said Fern, poking her dish towel into a cereal bowl.

'Fern,' said her mother sternly, 'you must not invent things. You know spiders don't tell stories. Spiders can't talk.'

'Charlotte can,' replied Fern. 'She doesn't

talk very loud, but she talks.'

'What kind of story did she tell?' asked Mrs Arable.

'Well,' began Fern, 'she told me about a cousin of hers who caught a fish in her web. Don't you think that's fascinating?'

'Fern, dear, how would a fish get in a spider's web?' said Mrs Arable. 'You know it couldn't happen. You're making this up.'

'Oh, it happened all right,' replied Fern. 'Charlotte never fibs. This cousin of hers built a web across a stream. One day she was hanging around on the web and a tiny fish leaped into the air and got tangled in the web. The fish was caught by one fin, Mother; its tail was wildly thrashing and shining in the sun. Can't you just see the web, sagging dangerously under the weight of the fish? Charlotte's cousin kept slipping in, dodging out, and she was beaten mercilessly over the head by the wildly thrashing fish, dancing in, dancing out, throwing . . .'

'Fern!' snapped her mother. 'Stop it! Stop inventing these wild tales!'

'I'm not inventing,' said Fern. 'I'm just telling you the facts.'

'What finally happened?' asked her mother, whose curiosity began to get the better of her.

'Charlotte's cousin won. She wrapped the fish up, then she ate him when she got good and ready. Spiders have to eat, the same as the rest of us.'

'Yes, I suppose they do,' said Mrs Arable, vaguely.

'Charlotte has another cousin who is a balloonist. She stands on her head, lets out a lot of line, and is carried aloft on the wind. Mother, wouldn't you simply love to do that?'

'Yes, I would, come to think of it,' replied Mrs Arable. 'But Fern, darling, I wish you would play outdoors today instead of going to Uncle Homer's barn. Find some of your playmates and do something nice outdoors. You're spending too much time in that barn – it isn't good for you to be alone so much.'

'Alone?' said Fern. 'Alone? My best friends are in the barn cellar. It is a very sociable place. Not at all lonely.'

Fern disappeared after a while, walking down the road towards Zuckermans. Her mother dusted the sitting-room. As she worked she kept thinking about Fern. It didn't seem natural for a little girl to be so interested in animals. Finally Mrs Arable made up her mind she would pay a call on old Dr Dorian and ask his advice. She got in the car and drove to his office in the village.

Dr Dorian had a thick beard. He was glad to see Mrs Arable and gave her a comfortable chair.

'It's about Fern,' she explained. 'Fern spends entirely too much time in the Zuckermans' barn. It doesn't seem normal. She sits on a milk stool in a corner of the barn cellar, near the pigpen, and watches animals, hour after hour. She just sits and listens.'

Dr Dorian leaned back and closed his eyes.

'How enchanting!' he said. 'It must be real nice and quiet down there. Homer has some sheep, hasn't he?'

'Yes,' said Mrs Arable. 'But it all started with that pig we let Fern raise on a bottle. She calls him Wilbur. Homer bought the pig, and ever since it left our place Fern has been going to her uncle's to be near it.'

'I've been hearing things about that pig,' said Dr Dorian, opening his eyes. 'They say he's quite a pig.'

'Have you heard about the words that appeared in the spider's web?' asked Mrs Arable nervously.

'Yes,' replied the doctor.

'Well, do you understand it?' asked Mrs Arable.

'Understand what?'

'Do you understand how there could be any writing in a spider's web?'

'Oh, no,' said Dr Dorian. 'I don't understand it. But for that matter I don't understand how a spider learned to spin a web in the first place. When the words appeared, everyone said they were a miracle. But nobody pointed out that the web itself is a miracle.'

'What's miraculous about a spider's web?' said Mrs Arable. 'I don't see why you say a web is a miracle – it's just a web.'

'Ever try to spin one?' asked Dr Dorian.

Mrs Arable shifted uneasily in her chair. 'No,' she replied. 'But I can crochet a doily and I can knit a sock.'

'Sure,' said the doctor. 'But somebody taught you, didn't they?'

'My mother taught me.'

'Well, who taught a spider? A young spider knows how to spin a web without any instructions from anybody. Don't you regard

that as a miracle?'

'I suppose so,' said Mrs Arable. 'I never looked at it that way before. Still, I don't understand how those words got into the web. I don't understand it, and I don't like what I can't understand.'

'None of us do,' said Dr Dorian, sighing. 'I'm a doctor. Doctors are supposed to understand everything. But I don't understand everything, and I don't intend to let it worry me.'

Mrs Arable fidgeted. 'Fern says the animals talk to each other. Dr Dorian, do you believe animals talk?'

'I never heard one say anything,' he replied. 'But that proves nothing. It is quite possible that an animal has spoken civilly to me and that I didn't catch the remark because I wasn't paying attention. Children pay better attention than grown-ups. If Fern says that the animals in Zuckerman's barn talk, I'm quite ready to believe her. Perhaps if people talked less, animals would talk more. People are incessant talkers – I can give you my word on that.'

'Well, I feel better about Fern,' said Mrs Arable. 'You don't think I need worry about her?'

'Does she look well?' asked the doctor.

'Oh, yes.'

'Appetite good?'

'Oh, yes, she's always hungry.'

'Sleep well at night?'

'Oh, yes.'

'Then don't worry,' said the doctor.

'Do you think she'll ever start thinking about something besides pigs and sheep and geese and spiders?'

'How old is Fern?'

'She's eight.'

'Well,' said Dr Dorian, 'I think she will always love animals. But I doubt that she spends her entire life in Homer Zuckerman's barn cellar. How about boys – does she know any boys?'

'She knows Henry Fussy,' said Mrs Arable brightly.

Dr Dorian closed his eyes again and went into deep thought. 'Henry Fussy,' he mumbled.

'Hmm. Remarkable. Well, I don't think you have anything to worry about. Let Fern associate with her friends in the barn if she wants to. I would say, offhand, that spiders and pigs were fully as interesting as Henry Fussy. Yet I predict that the day will come when even Henry will drop some chance remark that catches Fern's attention. It's amazing how children change from year to year. How's Avery?' he asked, opening his eyes wide.

'Oh, Avery,' chuckled Mrs Arable. 'Avery is always fine. Of course, he gets into poison ivy and gets stung by wasps and bees and brings frogs and snakes home and breaks everything he lays his hands on. He's fine.'

'Good!' said the doctor.

Mrs Arable said good-bye and thanked Dr Dorian very much for his advice. She felt greatly relieved.

Chapter Fifteen
The Crickets

The crickets sang in the grasses. They sang the song of summer's ending, a sad, monotonous song. 'Summer is over and gone,' they sang. 'Over and gone, over and gone. Summer is dying, dying.'

The crickets felt it was their duty to warn everybody that summertime cannot last for ever. Even on the most beautiful days in the whole year – the days when summer is changing into autumn – the crickets spread the rumour of sadness and change.

Everybody heard the song of the crickets. Avery and Fern Arable heard it as they walked the dusty road. They knew that school would soon begin again. The young geese heard it and knew that they would never be little goslings again. Charlotte heard it and knew that she hadn't much time left. Mrs Zuckerman, at work in the kitchen, heard the crickets, and a sadness came over her, too. 'Another summer gone,' she sighed. Lurvy, at work building a crate for Wilbur, heard the song and knew it was time to dig potatoes.

'Summer is over and gone,' repeated the crickets. 'How many nights till frost?' said the crickets. 'Good-bye, summer, good-bye, good-bye!'

The sheep heard the crickets, and they felt so uneasy they broke a hole in the pasture fence and wandered up into the field across the road. The gander discovered the hole and led his family through, and they walked to the orchard and ate the apples that were lying on the ground. A little maple tree in the swamp heard the cricket song and turned bright red with anxiety.

Wilbur was now the centre of attraction on the farm. Good food and regular hours were showing results: Wilbur was a pig any man would be proud of. One day more than a hundred people came to stand at his yard and admire him. Charlotte had written the word RADIANT, and Wilbur really looked radiant as he stood in the golden sunlight. Ever since the spider had befriended him, he had done his best to live up to his reputation. When Charlotte's web said SOME PIG, Wilbur had tried hard to look like some pig. When Charlotte's web said TERRIFIC, Wilbur had tried to look terrific. And now that the web said RADIANT, he did everything possible to make himself glow.

It is not easy to look radiant, but Wilbur threw himself into it with a will. He would turn his head slightly and blink his long eye-lashes. Then he would breathe deeply. And when his audience grew bored, he would spring into the air and do a back flip with a half twist. At this the crowd would yell and cheer. 'How's that for a pig?' Mr Zuckerman would ask, well pleased with himself. 'That pig is radiant.'

Some of Wilbur's friends in the barn worried for fear all this attention would go to his head and make him stuck up. But it never did. Wilbur was modest; fame did not spoil him. He still worried some about the future, as he could hardly believe that a mere spider would be able to save his life. Sometimes at night he would have a bad dream. He would dream that men were coming to get him with knives and guns. But that was only a dream. In the daytime, Wilbur usually felt happy and confident. No pig ever had truer friends, and he realized that friendship is one of the most satisfying things in the world. Even the song of the crickets did not make Wilbur too sad. He knew it was almost time for the County Fair, and he was looking forward to the trip. If he could distinguish himself at the Fair, and maybe win some prize money, he was sure Zuckerman would let him live.

Charlotte had worries of her own, but she kept quiet about them. One morning Wilbur asked her about the Fair.

'You're going *with* me, aren't you, Charlotte?' he said.

'Well, I don't know,' replied Charlotte. 'The Fair comes at a bad time for me. I shall find it inconvenient to leave home, even for a few days.'

'Why?' asked Wilbur.

'Oh, I just don't feel like leaving my web. Too much going on around here.'

'*Please* come with me!' begged Wilbur. 'I need you, Charlotte. I can't stand going to the Fair without you. You've just *got* to come.'

'No,' said Charlotte, 'I believe I'd better stay home and see if I can't get some work done.'

'What kind of work?' asked Wilbur.

'Egg laying. It's time I made an egg sac and filled it with eggs.'

'I didn't know you could lay eggs,' said Wilbur in amazement.

'Oh, sure,' said the spider. 'I'm versatile.'

'What does "versatile" mean – full of eggs?' asked Wilbur.

'Certainly not,' said Charlotte. ' "Versatile" means I can turn with ease from one thing to another. It means I don't have to limit my activities to spinning and trapping and stunts like that.'

'Why don't you come with me to the Fair Grounds and lay your eggs there?' pleaded Wilbur. 'It would be wonderful fun.'

Charlotte gave her web a twitch and moodily watched it sway. 'I'm afraid not,' she said. 'You don't know the first thing about egg laying, Wilbur. I can't arrange my family duties to suit the management of the County Fair. When I get ready to lay eggs, I have to lay eggs, Fair or no Fair. However, I don't want you to worry about it – you might lose weight. We'll leave it this way: I'll come to the Fair if I possibly can.'

'Oh, good!' said Wilbur. 'I knew you wouldn't forsake me just when I need you most.'

All that day Wilbur stayed inside, taking life easy in the straw. Charlotte rested and ate a grasshopper. She knew that she couldn't help Wilbur much longer. In a few days she would have to drop everything and build the beautiful little sac that would hold her eggs.

Chapter Sixteen
Off to the Fair

The night before the County Fair, everybody went to bed early. Fern and Avery were in bed by eight. Avery lay dreaming that the Ferris wheel had stopped and that he was in the top car. Fern lay dreaming that she was getting sick in the swings.

Lurvy was in bed by eight-thirty. He lay dreaming that he was throwing baseballs at a cloth cat and winning a genuine Navajo blanket. Mr and Mrs Zuckerman were in bed by nine. Mrs Zuckerman lay dreaming about a deep-freeze unit. Mr Zuckerman lay dreaming about Wilbur. He dreamt that Wilbur had grown until he was one hundred and sixteen

feet long and ninety-two feet high and that he had won all the prizes at the Fair and was covered with blue ribbons and even had a blue ribbon tied to the end of his tail.

Down in the barn cellar, the animals, too, went to sleep early, all except Charlotte. Tomorrow would be Fair Day. Every creature planned to get up early to see Wilbur off on his great adventure.

When morning came, everybody got up at daylight. The day was hot. Up the road at the Arables' house, Fern lugged a pail of hot water to her room and took a sponge bath. Then she put on her prettiest dress because she knew she would see boys at the Fair. Mrs Arable scrubbed the back of Avery's neck, and wet his hair, and parted it, and brushed it down hard till it stuck to the top of his head – all but about six hairs that stood straight up. Avery put on clean underwear, clean blue jeans, and a clean jersey. Mr Arable dressed, ate breakfast, and then went out and polished his truck. He had offered to drive everybody to the Fair, including Wilbur.

Bright and early, Lurvy put clean straw in Wilbur's crate and lifted it into the pigpen. The crate was green. In gold letters it said:

ZUCKERMAN'S FAMOUS PIG

Charlotte had her web looking fine for the occasion. Wilbur ate his breakfast slowly. He tried to look radiant without getting food in his ears.

In the kitchen, Mrs Zuckerman suddenly made an announcement.

'Homer,' she said to her husband, 'I am going to give that pig a buttermilk bath.'

'A what?' said Mr Zuckerman.

'A buttermilk bath. My grandmother used to bathe her pig with buttermilk when it got dirty – I just remembered.'

'Wilbur's not dirty,' said Mr Zuckerman proudly.

'He's filthy behind the ears,' said Mrs Zuckerman. 'Every time Lurvy slops him, the food runs down around the ears. Then it dries and forms a crust. He also has a smudge on one side where he lays in the manure.'

'He lays in clean straw,' corrected Mr Zuckerman.

'Well, he's dirty, and he's going to have a bath.'

Mr Zuckerman sat down weakly and ate a doughnut. His wife went to the woodshed.

When she returned, she wore rubber boots and an old raincoat, and she carried a bucket of buttermilk and a small wooden paddle.

'Edith, you're crazy,' mumbled Zuckerman.

But she paid no attention to him. Together they walked to the pigpen. Mrs Zuckerman wasted no time. She climbed in with Wilbur and went to work. Dipping her paddle in the buttermilk, she rubbed him all over. The geese gathered around to see the fun, and so did the sheep and lambs. Even Templeton poked his head out cautiously, to watch Wilbur get a buttermilk bath. Charlotte got so interested, she lowered herself on a dragline so she could see better. Wilbur stood still and closed his eyes. He could feel the buttermilk trickling down his sides. He opened his mouth and some buttermilk ran in. It was delicious. He felt radiant and happy. When Mrs Zuckerman got through and rubbed him dry, he was the cleanest, prettiest pig you ever saw. He was

pure white, pink around the ears and snout, and as smooth as silk.

The Zuckermans went up to change into their best clothes. Lurvy went to shave and put on his plaid shirt and his purple necktie. The animals were left to themselves in the barn.

The seven goslings paraded round and round their mother.

'Please, please, please take us to the Fair!' begged a gosling. Then all seven began teasing to go.

'Please, please, please, please, please, please . . .' They made quite a racket.

'Children!' snapped the goose. 'We're staying quietly-ietly-ietly at home. Only Wilbur-ilbur-ilbur is going to the Fair.'

Just then Charlotte interrupted.

'I shall go, too,' she said, softly. 'I have decided to go with Wilbur. He may need me. We can't tell what may happen at the Fair Grounds. Somebody's got to go along who knows how to write. And I think Templeton better come, too – I might need somebody to run errands and do general work.'

'I'm staying right here,' grumbled the rat. 'I haven't the slightest interest in fairs.'

'That's because you've never been to one,' remarked the old sheep. 'A fair is a rat's paradise. Everybody spills food at a fair. A rat can creep out late at night and have a feast. In the horse barn you will find oats that the trotters and pacers have spilled. In the trampled grass of the in-field you will find old discarded lunch-boxes containing the foul remains of peanut butter sandwiches, hard-boiled eggs, cracker crumbs, bits of doughnuts, and particles of cheese. In the hard-packed dirt of the midway, after the glaring lights are out and the people have gone home to bed, you will find a veritable treasure of popcorn fragments, frozen custard dribblings, candied apples abandoned by tired children, sugar fluff crystals, salted almonds, popsicles, partially gnawed ice cream cones, and the wooden sticks of lollypops. Everywhere is loot for a rat – in tents, in booths, in hay lofts – why, a fair has enough disgusting left-over food to satisfy a whole army of rats.'

Templeton's eyes were blazing.

'Is this true?' he asked. 'Is this appetizing yarn of yours true? I like high living, and what you say tempts me.'

'It is true,' said the old sheep. 'Go to the Fair,

Templeton. You will find that the conditions at a fair will surpass your wildest dreams. Buckets with sour mash sticking to them, tin cans containing particles of tuna fish, greasy paper bags stuffed with rotten . . .'

'That's enough!' cried Templeton. 'Don't tell me any more. I'm going.'

'Good,' said Charlotte, winking at the old sheep. 'Now then – there is no time to be lost. Wilbur will soon be put into the crate. Templeton and I must get in the crate right now and hide ourselves.'

The rat didn't waste a minute. He scampered over to the crate, crawled between the slats, and pulled straw up over him so he was hidden from sight.

'All right,' said Charlotte, 'I'm next.' She sailed into the air, let out a dragline, and dropped gently to the ground. Then she climbed the side of the crate and hid herself inside a knothole in the top board.

The old sheep nodded. 'What a cargo!' she said. 'That sign ought to say "Zuckerman's Famous Pig and Two Stowaways".'

'Look out, the people are coming-oming-oming!' shouted the gander. 'Cheese it, cheese it, cheese it!'

The big truck with Mr Arable at the wheel backed slowly down towards the barnyard. Lurvy and Mr Zuckerman walked alongside. Fern and Avery were standing in the body of the truck, hanging on to the sideboards.

'Listen to me,' whispered the old sheep to Wilbur. 'When they open the crate and try to put you in, struggle! Don't go without a struggle. Pigs always resist when they are being loaded.'

'If I struggle I'll get dirty,' said Wilbur.

'Never mind that – do as I say! Struggle! If you were to walk into the crate without resisting, Zuckerman might think you were bewitched. He'd be scared to go to the Fair.'

Templeton poked his head up through the straw. 'Struggle if you must,' said he, 'but kindly remember that I'm hiding down here in this crate and I don't want to be stepped on, or kicked in the face, or pummelled, or crushed in any way, or squashed, or buffeted about, or bruised, or lacerated, or scarred, or biffed. Just watch what you're doing, Mr Radiant, when they get shoving you in!'

'Be quiet, Templeton!' said the sheep. 'Pull in your head – they're coming. Look radiant, Wilbur! Lay low, Charlotte! Talk it up, geese!'

The truck backed slowly to the pigpen and stopped. Mr Arable cut the motor, got out, walked round to the rear, and lowered the tailgate. The geese cheered. Mrs Arable got out of the truck. Fern and Avery jumped to the ground. Mrs Zuckerman came walking down from the house. Everybody lined up at the fence and stood for a moment admiring Wilbur and the beautiful green crate. Nobody realized that the crate already contained a rat and a spider.

'That's some pig!' said Mrs Arable.

'He's terrific,' said Lurvy.

'He's very radiant,' said Fern, remembering the day he was born.

'Well,' said Mrs Zuckerman, 'he's clean, anyway. The buttermilk certainly helped.'

Mr Arable studied Wilbur carefully. 'Yes, he's a wonderful pig,' he said. 'It's hard to believe that he was the runt of the litter. You'll get some extra good ham and bacon, Homer, when it comes time to kill *that* pig.'

Wilbur heard these words and his heart almost stopped. 'I think I'm going to faint,' he whispered to the old sheep, who was watching.

'Kneel down!' whispered the old sheep. 'Let the blood rush to your head!'

Wilbur sank to his knees, all radiance gone. His eyes closed.

'Look!' screamed Fern. 'He's fading away!'

'Hey, watch me!' yelled Avery, crawling on

all fours into the crate. 'I'm a pig! I'm a pig!'

Avery's foot touched Templeton under the straw. 'What a mess!' thought the rat. 'What fantastic creatures boys are! Why did I let myself in for this?'

The geese saw Avery in the crate and cheered.

'Avery, you get out of that crate this instant!' commanded his mother. 'What do you think you are?'

'I'm a pig!' cried Avery, tossing handfuls of straw into the air. 'Oink, oink, oink!'

'The truck is rolling away, Papa,' said Fern.

The truck, with no one at the wheel, had started to roll downhill. Mr Arable dashed to the driver's seat and pulled on the emergency brake. The truck stopped. The geese cheered. Charlotte crouched and made herself as small as possible in the knothole, so Avery wouldn't see her.

'Come out at once!' cried Mrs Arable. Avery

crawled out of the crate on hands and knees, making faces at Wilbur. Wilbur fainted away.

'The pig has passed out,' said Mrs Zuckerman. 'Throw water on him!'

'Throw buttermilk!' suggested Avery.

The geese cheered.

Lurvy ran for a pail of water. Fern climbed into the pen and knelt by Wilbur's side.

'It's sunstroke,' said Zuckerman. 'The heat is too much for him.'

'Maybe he's dead,' said Avery.

'Come out of that pigpen *immediately*!' cried Mrs Arable. Avery obeyed his mother and climbed into the back of the truck so he could see better. Lurvy returned with cold water and dashed it on Wilbur.

'Throw some on me!' cried Avery. 'I'm hot, too.'

'Oh, keep quiet!' hollered Fern. 'Keep *qui*-ut!' Her eyes were brimming with tears.

Wilbur, feeling the cold water, came to. He

rose slowly to his feet, while
the geese cheered.

'He's up!' said Mr Arable. 'I guess there's
nothing wrong with him.'

'I'm hungry,' said Avery. 'I want a candied
apple.'

'Wilbur's all right now,' said Fern. 'We can
start. I want to take a ride in the Ferris wheel.'

Mr Zuckerman and Mr Arable and Lurvy
grabbed the pig and pushed him head-first
towards the crate. Wilbur began to struggle. The
harder the men pushed, the harder he held
back. Avery jumped down and joined the men.
Wilbur kicked and thrashed and grunted.
'Nothing wrong with this pig,' said Mr

Zuckerman cheerfully, pressing his knee against Wilbur's behind. 'All together, now, boys! Shove!'

With a final heave they jammed him into the crate. The geese cheered. Lurvy nailed some boards across the end, so Wilbur couldn't back out. Then, using all their strength, the men picked up the crate and heaved it aboard the truck. They did not know that under the straw was a rat, and inside a knot-hole was a big grey spider. They saw only a pig.

'Everybody in!' called Mr Arable. He started the motor. The ladies climbed in beside him. Mr Zuckerman and Lurvy and Fern and Avery rode in the back, hanging on to the sideboards. The truck began to move ahead. The geese cheered. The children answered their cheer, and away went everybody to the Fair.

Chapter Seventeen
Uncle

When they pulled into the Fair Grounds, they could hear music and see the Ferris wheel turning in the sky. They could smell the dust of the race-track where the sprinkling cart had moistened it; and they could smell hamburgers frying and see balloons aloft. They could hear sheep blatting in their pens. An enormous voice over the loudspeaker said: 'Attention, please! Will the owner of a Pontiac car, licence number H-2439, please move your car away from the fireworks shed!'

'Can I have some money?' asked Fern.

'Can I, too?' asked Avery.

'I'm going to win a doll by spinning a wheel

and it will stop at the right number,' said Fern.

'I'm going to steer a jet plane and make it bump into another one.'

'Can I have a balloon?' asked Fern.

'Can I have a frozen custard and a cheeseburger and some raspberry soda pop?' asked Avery.

'You children be quiet till we get the pig unloaded,' said Mrs Arable.

'Let's let the children go off by themselves,' suggested Mr Arable. 'The Fair only comes once a year.' Mr Arable gave Fern two quarters and two dimes. He gave Avery five dimes and four nickels. 'Now run along!' he said. 'And remember, the money has to last *all day*. Don't spend it all the first few minutes. And be back here at the truck at noontime so we can all have lunch together. And don't eat a lot of stuff that's going to make you sick to your stomachs.'

'And if you go in those swings,' said Mrs

Arable, 'you hang on tight! You hang on *very* tight. Hear me?'

'And don't get lost!' said Mrs Zuckerman.

'And don't get dirty!'

'Don't get overheated!' said their mother.

'Watch out for pickpockets!' cautioned their father.

'And don't cross the race-track when the horses are coming!' cried Mrs Zuckerman.

The children grabbed each other by the hand and danced off in the direction of the merry-go-round, towards the wonderful music and the wonderful adventure and the wonderful excitement, into the wonderful midway where there would be no parents to guard them and guide them, and where they could be happy and free and do as they pleased. Mrs Arable stood quietly and watched them go. Then she sighed. Then she blew her nose.

'Do you really think it's all right?' she asked.

'Well, they've got to grow up some time,'

said Mr Arable. 'And a fair is a good place to start, I guess.'

While Wilbur was being unloaded and taken out of his crate and into his new pigpen, crowds gathered to watch. They stared at the sign

ZUCKERMAN'S FAMOUS PIG. Wilbur stared back and tried to look extra good. He was pleased with his new home. The pen was grassy, and it was shaded from the sun by a shed roof.

Charlotte, watching her chance, scrambled out of the crate and climbed a post to the under side of the roof. Nobody noticed her.

Templeton, not wishing to come out in broad daylight, stayed quietly under the straw at the bottom of the crate. Mr Zuckerman poured some skim milk into Wilbur's trough, pitched clean straw into his pen, and then he and Mrs Zuckerman and the Arables walked away towards the cattle barn to look at purebred cows and to see the sights. Mr Zuckerman particularly wanted to look at tractors. Mrs Zuckerman wanted to see a deep freeze. Lurvy wandered off by himself, hoping to meet friends and have some fun on the midway.

As soon as the people were gone, Charlotte spoke to Wilbur.

'It's a good thing you can't see what I see,' she said.

'What do you see?' asked Wilbur.

'There's a pig in the next pen and he's enormous. I'm afraid he's much bigger than you are.'

'Maybe he's older than I am, and has had more time to grow,' suggested Wilbur. Tears began to come to his eyes.

'I'll drop down and have a closer look,' Charlotte said. Then she crawled along a beam till she was directly over the next pen. She let herself down on a dragline until she hung in the air just in front of the big pig's snout.

'May I have your name?' she asked, politely.

The pig stared at her. 'No name,' he said in a big, hearty voice. 'Just call me Uncle.'

'Very well, Uncle,' replied Charlotte. 'What is the date of your birth? Are you a spring pig?'

'Sure I'm a spring pig,' replied Uncle. 'What did you think I was, a spring chicken? Haw, haw – that's a good one, eh, sister?'

'Mildly funny,' said Charlotte. 'I've heard funnier ones though. Glad to have met you, and now I must be going.'

She ascended slowly and returned to Wilbur's pen.

'He claims he's a spring pig,' reported Charlotte, 'and perhaps he is. One thing is certain, he has a most unattractive personality. He is too familiar, too noisy, and he cracks weak jokes. Also, he's not anywhere near as clean as you are, nor as pleasant. I took quite a dislike to him in our brief interview. He's going to be a hard pig to beat, though, Wilbur, on account of his size and weight. But with me helping you, it can be done.'

'When are you going to spin a web?' asked Wilbur.

'This afternoon, late, if I'm not too tired,' said

Charlotte. 'The least thing tires me these days. I don't seem to have the energy I once had. My age, I guess.'

Wilbur looked at his friend. She looked rather swollen and seemed listless.

'I'm awfully sorry to hear that you're feeling poorly, Charlotte,' he said. 'Perhaps if you spin a web and catch a couple of flies you'll feel better.'

'Perhaps,' she said, wearily. 'But I feel like the end of a long day.' Clinging upside down to the ceiling, she settled down for a nap, leaving Wilbur very much worried.

All morning people wandered past Wilbur's

pen. Dozens and dozens of strangers stopped to stare at him and to admire his silky white coat, his curly tail, his kind and radiant expression. Then they would move on to the next pen where the bigger pig lay. Wilbur heard several people make favourable remarks about Uncle's great size. He couldn't help overhearing these remarks, and he couldn't help worrying. 'And now, with Charlotte not feeling well . . .' he thought. 'Oh, dear!'

All morning Templeton slept quietly under the straw. The day grew fiercely hot. At noon the Zuckermans and the Arables returned to the pigpen. Then, a few minutes later, Fern and Avery showed up. Fern had a monkey doll in her arms and was eating Krackerjack. Avery had a balloon tied to his ear and was chewing a candied apple. The children were hot and dirty.

'Isn't it hot?' said Mrs Zuckerman.

'It's *terribly* hot,' said Mrs Arable, fanning herself with an advertisement of a deep freeze.

One by one they climbed into the truck and opened lunchboxes. The sun beat down on everything. Nobody seemed hungry.

'When are the judges going to decide about Wilbur?' asked Mrs Zuckerman.

'Not till tomorrow,' said Mr Zuckerman.

Lurvy appeared, carrying an Indian blanket that he had won.

'That's just what we need,' said Avery. 'A blanket.'

'Of course it is,' replied Lurvy. And he spread the blanket across the sideboards of the truck so that it was like a little tent. The children sat in the shade, under the blanket, and felt better.

After lunch, they stretched out and fell asleep.

Chapter Eighteen

The Cool
of the Evening

In the cool of the evening, when shadows darkened the Fair Grounds, Templeton crept from the crate and looked around. Wilbur lay asleep in the straw. Charlotte was building a web. Templeton's keen nose detected many fine smells in the air. The rat was hungry and thirsty. He decided to go exploring. Without saying anything to anybody, he started off.

'Bring me back a word!' Charlotte called after him. 'I shall be writing tonight for the last time.'

The rat mumbled something to himself and disappeared into the shadows. He did not like being treated like a messenger boy.

After the heat of the day, the evening came as

a welcome relief to all. The Ferris wheel was lighted now. It went round and round in the sky and seemed twice as high as by day. There were lights on the midway, and you could hear the crackle of the gambling machines and the music of the merry-go-round and the voice of the man in the beano booth calling numbers.

The children felt refreshed after their nap. Fern met her friend Henry Fussy, and he invited her to ride with him in the Ferris wheel. He even bought a ticket for her, so it didn't cost her anything. When Mrs Arable happened to look up into the starry sky and saw her little daughter sitting with Henry Fussy and going higher and higher into the air, and saw how happy Fern looked, she just shook her head. 'My, my!' she said. 'Henry Fussy. Think of that!'

Templeton kept out of sight. In the tall grass behind the cattle barn he found a folded newspaper. Inside it were left-overs from somebody's lunch: a devilled ham sandwich, a

piece of Swiss cheese, part of a hard-boiled egg, and the core of a wormy apple. The rat crawled in and ate everything. Then he tore a word out of the paper, rolled it up, and started back to Wilbur's pen.

Charlotte had her web almost finished when Templeton returned, carrying the newspaper clipping. She had left a space in the middle of the web. At this hour, no people were round the pigpen, so the rat and the spider and the pig were by themselves.

'I hope you brought a good one,' Charlotte said. 'It is the last word I shall ever write.'

'Here,' said Templeton, unrolling the paper.

'What does it say?' asked Charlotte. 'You'll have to read it for me.'

'It says HUMBLE,' replied the rat.

'Humble?' said Charlotte. ' "Humble" has two meanings. It means "not proud" and it means "near the ground". That's Wilbur all over. He's not proud and he's near the ground.'

'Well, I hope you're satisfied,' sneered the rat. 'I'm not going to spend all my time fetching and carrying. I came to this Fair to enjoy myself, not to deliver papers.'

'You've been very helpful,' Charlotte said. 'Run along, if you want to see more of the Fair.'

The rat grinned. 'I'm going to make a night of it,' he said. 'The old sheep was right – this Fair is a rat's paradise. What eating! And what drinking! And everywhere good hiding and good hunting. Bye-bye, my humble Wilbur! Fare thee well, Charlotte, you old schemer! This will be a night to remember in a rat's life.'

He vanished into the shadows.

Charlotte went back to her work. It was quite dark now. In the distance, fireworks began going off – rockets, scattering fiery balls in the sky. By the time the Arables and the Zuckermans and Lurvy returned from the grandstand, Charlotte had finished her web. The word HUMBLE was woven neatly in the centre. Nobody noticed it in the darkness. Everyone was tired and happy.

Fern and Avery climbed into the truck and lay down. They pulled the Indian blanket over them. Lurvy gave Wilbur a forkful of fresh straw. Mr Arable patted him. 'Time for us to go home,' he said to the pig. 'See you tomorrow.'

The grown-ups climbed slowly into the truck and Wilbur heard the engine start and then heard the truck moving away in low speed. He would have felt lonely and homesick, had Charlotte not been with him. He never felt lonely when she was near. In the distance he could still hear the music of the merry-go-round.

As he was dropping off to sleep he spoke to Charlotte.

'Sing me that song again, about the dung and the dark,' he begged.

'Not tonight,' she said in a low voice. 'I'm too tired.' Her voice didn't seem to come from her web.

'Where are you?' asked Wilbur. 'I can't see you. Are you on your web?'

'I'm back here,' she answered. 'Up in this back corner.'

'Why aren't you on your web?' asked Wilbur. 'You almost never leave your web.'

'I've left it tonight,' she said.

Wilbur closed his eyes. 'Charlotte,' he said, after a while, 'do you really think Zuckerman will let me live and not kill me when the cold weather comes? Do you really think so?'

'Of course,' said Charlotte. 'You are a famous pig and you are a good pig. Tomorrow you will probably win a prize. The whole world will hear about you. Zuckerman will be proud and happy to own such a pig. You have nothing to fear, Wilbur – nothing to worry about. Maybe you'll live for ever – who knows? And now, go to sleep.'

For a while there was no sound. Then Wilbur's voice:

'What are you doing up there, Charlotte?'

'Oh, making something,' she said. 'Making something, as usual.'

'Is it something for me?' asked Wilbur.

'No,' said Charlotte. 'It's something for *me*, for a change.'

'Please tell me what it is,' begged Wilbur.

'I'll tell you in the morning,' she said. 'When the first light comes into the sky and the sparrows stir and the cows rattle their chains, when the rooster crows and the stars fade, when early cars whisper along the highway, you look up here and I'll show you something. I will show you my masterpiece.'

Before she finished the sentence, Wilbur was asleep. She could tell by the sound of his breathing that he was sleeping peacefully, deep in the straw.

Miles away, at the Arables' house, the men sat round the kitchen table eating a dish of canned peaches and talking over the events of the day. Upstairs, Avery was already in bed and asleep. Mrs Arable was tucking Fern into bed.

'Did you have a good time at the Fair?' she asked as she kissed her daughter.

Fern nodded. 'I had the best time I have ever had anywhere or any time in all of my whole life.'

'Well!' said Mrs Arable. 'Isn't that nice.'

Chapter Nineteen
The Egg Sac

Next morning when the first light came into the sky and the sparrows stirred in the trees, when the cows rattled their chains and the rooster crowed and the early automobiles went whispering along the road, Wilbur awoke and looked for Charlotte. He saw her up overhead in a corner near the back of his pen. She was very quiet. Her eight legs were spread wide. She seemed to have shrunk during the night. Next to her, attached to the ceiling, Wilbur saw a curious object. It was a sort of sac, or cocoon. It was peach-coloured and looked as though it were made of cotton candy.

'Are you awake, Charlotte?' he said softly.

'Yes,' came the answer.

'What is that nifty little thing? Did you make it?'

'I did indeed,' replied Charlotte in a weak voice.

'Is it a plaything?'

'Plaything? I should say not. It is my egg sac, my *magnum opus*.'

'I don't know what a *magnum opus* is,' said Wilbur.

'That's Latin,' explained Charlotte. 'It means "great work". This egg sac is my great work — the finest thing I have ever made.'

'What's inside it?' asked Wilbur. 'Eggs?'

'Five hundred and fourteen of them,' she replied.

'Five *hundred* and *fourteen*?' said Wilbur. 'You're kidding.'

'No, I'm not. I counted them. I got started counting, so I kept on — just to keep my mind occupied.'

'It's a perfectly beautiful egg sac,' said Wilbur, feeling as happy as though he had constructed it himself.

'Yes, it *is* pretty,' replied Charlotte, patting the sac with her two front legs. 'Anyway, I can guarantee that it is strong. It's made out of the toughest material I have. It is also waterproof. The eggs are inside and will be warm and dry.'

'Charlotte,' said Wilbur dreamily, 'are you really going to have five hundred and fourteen children?'

'If nothing happens, yes,' she said. 'Of course, they won't show up till next spring.'

Wilbur noticed that Charlotte's voice sounded sad.

'What makes you sound so down-hearted? I should think you'd be terribly happy about this.'

'Oh, don't pay any attention to me,' said Charlotte. 'I just don't have much pep any more. I guess I feel sad because I won't ever see my children.'

'What do you mean you won't see your children! Of *course* you will. We'll *all* see them. It's going to be simply wonderful next spring in the barn cellar with five hundred and fourteen baby spiders running around all over the place. And the geese will have a new set of goslings, and the sheep will have their new lambs . . .'

'Maybe,' said Charlotte quietly. 'However, I have a feeling I'm not going to see the results of last night's efforts. I don't feel good at all. I think I'm languishing, to tell you the truth.'

Wilbur didn't understand the word

'languish' and he hated to bother Charlotte by asking her to explain. But he was so worried he felt he had to ask.

'What does "languishing" mean?'

'It means I'm slowing up, feeling my age. I'm not young any more, Wilbur. But I don't want you to worry about me. This is your big day today. Look at my web – doesn't it show up well with the dew on it?'

Charlotte's web never looked more beautiful than it looked this morning. Each strand held dozens of bright drops of early morning dew. The light from the east struck it and made it all plain and clear. It was a perfect piece of designing and building. In another hour or two, a steady stream of people would pass by, admiring it, and reading it, and looking at Wilbur, and marvelling at the miracle.

As Wilbur was studying the web, a pair of whiskers and a sharp face appeared. Slowly Templeton dragged himself across the pen and threw himself down in a corner.

'I'm back,' he said in a husky voice. 'What a night!'

The rat was swollen to twice his normal size. His stomach was as big round as a jelly jar.

'What a night!' he repeated, hoarsely. 'What feasting and carousing! A real gorge! I must have eaten the remains of thirty lunches. Never have I seen such leavings, and everything well ripened and seasoned with the passage of time

and the heat of the day. Oh, it was rich, my friends, rich!'

'You ought to be ashamed of yourself,' said

Charlotte in disgust. 'It would serve you right if you had an acute attack of indigestion.'

'Don't worry about my stomach,' snarled Templeton. 'It can handle anything. And by the way, I've got some bad news. As I came past that pig next door – the one that calls himself Uncle – I noticed a blue tag on the front of his pen. That means he has won first prize. I guess you're licked, Wilbur. You might as well relax – nobody is going to hang any medal on *you*. Furthermore, I wouldn't be surprised if Zuckerman changes his mind about you. Wait till he gets hankering for some fresh pork and smoked ham and crisp bacon! He'll take the knife to you, my boy.'

'Be still, Templeton!' said Charlotte. 'You're too stuffed and bloated to know what you're saying. Don't pay any attention to him, Wilbur!'

Wilbur tried not to think about what the rat had just said. He decided to change the subject.

'Templeton,' said Wilbur, 'if you weren't so

dopey, you would have noticed that Charlotte has made an egg sac. She is going to become a mother. For your information, there are five hundred and fourteen eggs in that peachy little sac.'

'Is this true?' asked the rat, eyeing the sac suspiciously.

'Yes, it's true,' sighed Charlotte.

'Congratulations!' murmured Templeton. 'This has been a night!' He closed his eyes, pulled some straw over himself, and dropped off into a deep sleep. Wilbur and Charlotte were glad to be rid of him for a while.

At nine o'clock, Mr Arable's truck rolled into the Fair Grounds and came to a stop at Wilbur's pen. Everybody climbed out.

'Look!' cried Fern. 'Look at Charlotte's web! Look what it says!'

The grown-ups and the children joined hands and stood there, studying the new sign.

'HUMBLE,' said Mr Zuckerman. 'Now isn't that just the word for Wilbur!'

Everyone rejoiced to find that the miracle of the web had been repeated. Wilbur gazed up lovingly into their faces. He looked very humble and very grateful. Fern winked at Charlotte. Lurvy soon got busy. He poured a bucket of warm slops into the trough, and while Wilbur ate his breakfast Lurvy scratched him gently with a smooth stick.

'Wait a minute!' cried Avery. 'Look at this!' He pointed to the blue tag on Uncle's pen. 'This pig has won first prize already.'

The Zuckermans and the Arables stared at the tag. Mrs Zuckerman began to cry. Nobody said a word. They just stared at the tag. Then they stared at Uncle. Then they stared at the tag again. Lurvy took out an enormous handkerchief and blew his nose very loud – so loud, in fact, that the noise was heard by stableboys over at the horse barn.

'Can I have some money?' asked Fern. 'I want to go out on the midway.'

'You stay right where you are!' said her mother. Tears came to Fern's eyes.

'What's everybody crying about?' asked Mr Zuckerman. 'Let's get busy! Edith, bring the buttermilk!'

Mrs Zuckerman wiped her eyes with her handkerchief. She went to the truck and came back with a gallon jar of buttermilk.

'Bath time!' said Zuckerman, cheerfully. He and Mrs Zuckerman and Avery climbed into Wilbur's pen. Avery slowly poured buttermilk on Wilbur's head and back, and as it trickled down his sides and cheeks, Mr and Mrs Zuckerman rubbed it into his hair and skin. Passers-by stopped to watch. Pretty soon quite a crowd had gathered. Wilbur grew beautifully white and smooth. The morning sun shone through his pink ears.

'He isn't as big as that pig next door,'

remarked one bystander, 'but he's cleaner. That's what I like.'

'So do I,' said another man.

'He's humble, too,' said a woman, reading the sign on the web.

Everybody who visited the pigpen had a good word to say about Wilbur. Everyone admired the web. And of course nobody noticed Charlotte.

Suddenly a voice was heard on the loudspeaker.

'Attention, please!' it said. 'Will Mr Homer Zuckerman bring his famous pig to the judges' booth in front of the grandstand. A special award will be made there in twenty minutes. Everyone is invited to attend. Crate your pig, please, Mr Zuckerman, and report to the judges' booth promptly!'

For a moment after this announcement, the Arables and the Zuckermans were unable to speak or move. Then Avery picked up a handful

of straw and threw it high in the air and gave a
loud yell. The straw fluttered down like confetti
into Fern's hair. Mr Zuckerman hugged Mrs
Zuckerman. Mr Arable kissed Mrs Arable.

Avery kissed Wilbur. Lurvy shook hands with everybody. Fern hugged her mother. Avery hugged Fern. Mrs Arable hugged Mrs Zuckerman.

Up overhead, in the shadows of the ceiling, Charlotte crouched unseen, her front legs encircling her egg sac. Her heart was not beating as strongly as usual and she felt weary and old, but she was sure at last that she had saved Wilbur's life, and she felt peaceful and contented.

'We have no time to lose!' shouted Mr Zuckerman. 'Lurvy, help with the crate!'

'Can I have some money?' asked Fern.

'You *wait*!' said Mrs Arable. 'Can't you see everybody is busy?'

'Put that empty buttermilk jar into the truck!' commanded Mr Arable. Avery grabbed the jar and rushed to the truck.

'Does my hair look all right?' asked Mrs Zuckerman.

'Looks fine,' snapped Mr Zuckerman, as he and Lurvy set the crate down in front of Wilbur.

'You didn't even *look* at my hair!' said Mrs Zuckerman.

'You're all right, Edith,' said Mrs Arable. 'Just keep calm.'

Templeton, asleep in the straw, heard the commotion and awoke. He didn't know exactly what was going on, but when he saw the men shoving Wilbur into the crate he made up his mind to go along. He watched his chance and, when no one was looking, he crept into the crate and buried himself in the straw at the bottom.

'All ready, boys!' cried Mr Zuckerman. 'Let's go!' He and Mr Arable and Lurvy and Avery grabbed the crate and boosted it over the side of the pen and up into the truck. Fern jumped aboard and sat on top of the crate. She still had straw in her hair and looked very pretty and excited. Mr Arable started the motor. Everyone climbed in, and off they drove to the judges' booth in front of the grandstand.

As they passed the Ferris wheel, Fern gazed up at it and wished she were in the topmost car with Henry Fussy at her side.

Chapter Twenty

The Hour of Triumph

'Special announcement!' said the loudspeaker in a pompous voice. 'The management of the Fair takes great pleasure in presenting Mr Homer L. Zuckerman and his famous pig. The truck bearing this extraordinary animal is now approaching the infield. Kindly stand back and give the truck room to proceed! In a few moments the pig will be unloaded in the special judging ring in front of the grandstand, where a special award will be made. Will the crowd please make way and let the truck pass. Thank you.'

Wilbur trembled when he heard this speech. He felt happy but dizzy. The truck crept along slowly in low speed. Crowds of people surrounded it, and Mr Arable had to drive very carefully in order not to run over anybody. At last he managed to reach the judges' stand. Avery jumped out and lowered the tailgate.

'I'm scared to death,' whispered Mrs Zuckerman. 'Hundreds of people are looking at us.'

'Cheer up,' replied Mrs Arable, 'this is fun.'

'Unload your pig, please!' said the loudspeaker.

'Altogether, now, boys!' said Mr Zuckerman. Several men stepped forward from the crowd to help lift the crate. Avery was the busiest helper of all.

'Tuck your shirt in, Avery!' cried Mrs Zuckerman. 'And tighten your belt. Your pants are coming down.'

'Can't you see I'm busy?' replied Avery in disgust.

'Look!' cried Fern, pointing. 'There's Henry!'

'Don't shout, Fern!' said her mother. 'And don't point!'

'Can't I *please* have some money?' asked Fern. 'Henry invited me to go on the Ferris wheel again, only I don't think he has any money left. He ran out of money.'

Mrs Arable opened her handbag. 'Here,' she said. 'Here is forty cents. Now don't get lost! And be back at our regular meeting-place by the pigpen very soon!'

Fern raced off, ducking and dodging through the crowd, in search of Henry.

'The Zuckerman pig is now being taken from his crate,' boomed the voice of the loudspeaker. 'Stand by for an announcement!'

Templeton crouched under the straw at the bottom of the crate. 'What a lot of nonsense!' muttered the rat. 'What a lot of fuss about nothing!'

Over in the pigpen, silent and alone,

Charlotte rested. Her two front legs embraced the egg sac. Charlotte could hear everything that was said on the loudspeaker. The words gave her courage. This was her hour of triumph.

As Wilbur came out of the crate, the crowd clapped and cheered. Mr Zuckerman took off his cap and bowed. Lurvy pulled his big handkerchief from his pocket and wiped the sweat from the back of his neck. Avery knelt in the dirt by Wilbur's side, busily stroking him and showing off. Mrs Zuckerman and Mrs Arable stood on the running board of the truck.

'Ladeez and gentlemen,' said the loudspeaker, 'we now present Mr Homer L. Zuckerman's distinguished pig. The fame of this unique animal has spread to the far corners of the earth, attracting many valuable tourists to our great State. Many of you will recall that never-to-be-forgotten day last summer when the writing appeared mysteriously on the spider's web in Mr Zuckerman's barn, calling the attention of all and sundry to the fact that this pig was completely out of the ordinary. This miracle has never been fully explained, although learned men have visited the Zuckerman pigpen to study and observe the phenomenon. In the last analysis, we simply know that we are dealing with supernatural forces here, and we should all feel proud and grateful. In the words of the spider's web, ladies and gentlemen, this is some pig.'

Wilbur blushed. He stood perfectly still and tried to look his best.

'This magnificent animal,' continued the loud-speaker, 'is truly terrific. Look at him, ladies and gentlemen! Note the smoothness and whiteness of the coat, observe the spotless skin, the healthy pink glow of ears and snout.'

'It's the buttermilk,' whispered Mrs Arable to Mrs Zuckerman.

'Note the general radiance of this animal! Then remember the day when the word "radiant" appeared clearly on the web. Whence came this mysterious writing? Not from the spider, we can rest assured of that. Spiders are very clever at weaving their webs, but needless to say spiders cannot write.'

'Oh, they can't, can't they?' murmured Charlotte to herself.

'Ladeez and gentlemen,' continued the loudspeaker, 'I must not take any more of your valuable time. On behalf of the governors of the Fair, I have the honour of awarding a special prize of twenty-five dollars to Mr Zuckerman, together with a handsome bronze medal suitably engraved, in token of our appreciation of the part played by this pig – this radiant, this terrific, this humble pig – in attracting so many visitors to our great County Fair.'

Wilbur had been feeling dizzier and dizzier through this long, complimentary speech.

When he heard the crowd begin to cheer and clap again, he suddenly fainted away. His legs collapsed, his mind went blank, and he fell to the ground, unconscious.

'What's wrong?' asked the loudspeaker. 'What's going on, Zuckerman? What's the trouble with your pig?'

Avery was kneeling by Wilbur's head, stroking him. Mr Zuckerman was dancing about, fanning him with his cap.

'He's all right,' cried Mr Zuckerman. 'He gets these spells. He's modest and can't stand praise.'

'Well, we can't give a prize to a *dead* pig,' said the loudspeaker. 'It's never been done.'

'He isn't dead,' hollered Zuckerman. 'He's fainted. He gets embarrassed easily. Run for some water, Lurvy!'

Lurvy sprang from the judges' ring and disappeared.

Templeton poked his head from the straw.

He noticed that the end of Wilbur's tail was within reach. Templeton grinned. 'I'll tend to this,' he chuckled. He took Wilbur's tail in his mouth and bit it, just as hard as he could bite. The pain revived Wilbur. In a flash he was back on his feet.

'Ouch!' he screamed.

'Hoorray!' yelled the crowd. 'He's up! The pig's up! Good work, Zuckerman! That's some pig!' Everyone was delighted. Mr Zuckerman was the most pleased of all. He sighed with relief. Nobody had seen Templeton. The rat had done his work well.

And now one of the judges climbed into the ring with the prizes. He handed Mr Zuckerman two ten-dollar bills and a five-dollar bill. Then he tied the medal around Wilbur's neck. Then he shook hands with Mr Zuckerman while Wilbur blushed. Avery put out his hand and the judge shook hands with him, too. The crowd cheered. A photographer took Wilbur's picture.

A great feeling of happiness swept over the Zuckermans and the Arables. This was the greatest moment in Mr Zuckerman's life. It is deeply satisfying to win a prize in front of a lot of people.

As Wilbur was being shoved back into the crate, Lurvy came charging through the crowd carrying a pail of water. His eyes had a wild look. Without hesitating a second, he dashed the water at Wilbur. In his excitement he missed his aim, and the water splashed all over Mr Zuckerman and Avery. They got soaking wet.

'For goodness' sake!' bellowed Mr Zuckerman, who was really drenched. 'What ails you, Lurvy? Can't you see the pig is all right?'

'You asked for water,' said Lurvy meekly.

'I didn't ask for a shower bath,' said Mr Zuckerman. The crowd roared with laughter. Finally Mr Zuckerman had to laugh, too. And of course Avery was tickled to find himself so wet, and he immediately started to act like a clown. He pretended he was taking a shower bath; he made faces and danced around and rubbed imaginary soap under his armpits. Then he dried himself with an imaginary towel.

'Avery, stop it!' cried his mother. 'Stop showing off!'

But the crowd loved it. Avery heard nothing but the applause. He liked being a clown in a ring, with everybody watching, in front of a grandstand. When he discovered there was still a little water left in the bottom of the pail, he raised the pail high in the air and dumped the water on himself and made faces. The children in the grandstand screamed with appreciation.

At last things calmed down. Wilbur was loaded into the truck. Avery was led from the ring by his mother and placed on the seat of the truck to dry off. The truck, driven by Mr Arable, crawled slowly back to the pigpen. Avery's wet trousers made a big wet spot on the seat.

Chapter Twenty-One
Last Day

Charlotte and Wilbur were alone. The families had gone to look for Fern. Templeton was asleep. Wilbur lay resting after the excitement and strain of the ceremony. His medal still hung from his neck; by looking out of the corner of his eye he could see it.

'Charlotte,' said Wilbur after a while, 'why are you so quiet?'

'I like to sit still,' she said. 'I've always been rather quiet.'

'Yes, but you seem specially so today. Do you feel all right?'

'A little tired, perhaps. But I feel peaceful. Your success in the ring this morning was, to a small degree, my success. Your future is assured. You will live, secure and safe, Wilbur. Nothing can harm you now. These autumn days will shorten and grow cold. The leaves will shake loose from the trees and fall. Christmas will come, then the snows of winter. You will live to enjoy the beauty of the frozen world, for you mean a great deal to Zuckerman and he will not harm you, ever. Winter will pass, the days will lengthen, the ice will melt in the pasture pond. The song sparrow will return and sing, the frogs will awake, the warm wind will blow again. All these sights and sounds and smells will be yours to enjoy, Wilbur – this lovely world, these golden days . . .'

Charlotte stopped. A moment later a tear came to Wilbur's eye. 'Oh, Charlotte,' he said. 'To think that when I first met you I thought you were cruel and bloodthirsty!'

When he recovered from his emotion, he spoke again.

'Why did you do all this for me?' he asked. 'I don't deserve it. I've never done anything for you.'

'You have been my friend,' replied Charlotte. 'That in itself is a tremendous thing. I wove my webs for you because I liked you. After all, what's a life, anyway? We're born, we live a little while, we die. A spider's life can't help being something of a mess, with all this trapping and eating flies. By helping you, perhaps I was trying to lift up my life a trifle. Heaven knows anyone's life can stand a little of that.'

'Well,' said Wilbur, 'I'm no good at making speeches. I haven't got your gift for words. But you have saved me, Charlotte, and I would gladly give my life for you – I really would.'

'I'm sure you would. And I thank you for your generous sentiments.'

'Charlotte,' said Wilbur. 'We're all going home today. The Fair is almost over. Won't it be wonderful to be back home in the barn cellar again with the sheep and the geese? Aren't you anxious to get home?'

For a moment Charlotte said nothing. Then she spoke in a voice so low Wilbur could hardly hear the words.

'I will not be going back to the barn,' she said.

Wilbur leapt to his feet. 'Not going back?' he cried. 'Charlotte, what are you talking about?'

'I'm done for,' she replied. 'In a day or two I'll be dead. I haven't even strength enough to climb down into the crate. I doubt if I have enough silk in my spinneret to lower me to the ground.'

Hearing this, Wilbur threw himself down in an agony of pain and sorrow. Great sobs racked his body. He heaved and grunted with desolation. 'Charlotte,' he moaned. 'Charlotte! My true friend!'

'Come now, let's not make a scene,' said the spider. 'Be quiet, Wilbur. Stop thrashing about!'

Last Day 219

'But I can't *stand* it,' shouted Wilbur. 'I won't leave you here alone to die. If you're going to stay here I shall stay, too.'

'Don't be ridiculous,' said Charlotte. 'You can't stay here. Zuckerman and Lurvy and John Arable and the others will be back any minute now, and they'll shove you into that crate and away you'll go. Besides, it wouldn't make any sense for you to stay. There would be no one to feed you. The Fair Grounds will soon be empty and deserted.'

Wilbur was in a panic. He raced round and round the pen. Suddenly he had an idea – he thought of the egg sac and the five hundred and fourteen little spiders that would hatch in the spring. If Charlotte herself was unable to go home to the barn, at least he must take her children along.

Wilbur rushed to the front of his pen. He put his front feet up on the top board and gazed around. In the distance he saw the Arables and the Zuckermans approaching. He knew he would have to act quickly.

'Where's Templeton?' he demanded.

'He's in that corner, under the straw, asleep,' said Charlotte.

Wilbur rushed over, pushed his strong snout under the rat, and tossed him into the air.

'Templeton!' screamed Wilbur. 'Pay attention!'

The rat, surprised out of a sound sleep, looked first dazed then disgusted.

'What kind of monkeyshine is this?' he growled. 'Can't a rat catch a wink of sleep without being rudely popped into the air?'

'Listen to me!' cried Wilbur. 'Charlotte is very ill. She has only a short time to live. She cannot accompany us home, because of her condition. Therefore, it is absolutely necessary that I take her egg sac with me. I can't reach it, and I can't climb. You are the only one that can get it. There's not a second to be lost. The people are coming – they'll be here in no time. Please, please, *please*, Templeton, climb up and get the egg sac.'

The rat yawned. He straightened his whiskers. Then he looked up at the egg sac.

'So!' he said, in disgust. 'So it's old Templeton to the rescue again, is it? Templeton do this, Templeton do that, Templeton please run down to the dump and get me a magazine clipping, Templeton please lend me a piece of string so I can spin a web.'

'Oh, hurry!' said Wilbur. 'Hurry up, Templeton!'

But the rat was in no hurry. He began imitating Wilbur's voice.

'So it's "Hurry up, Templeton", is it?' he said. 'Ho, ho. And what thanks do I ever get for these services, I would like to know? Never a kind word for old Templeton, only abuse and wisecracks and side remarks. Never a kind word for a rat.'

'Templeton,' said Wilbur in desperation, 'if you don't stop talking and get busy, all will be lost, and I will die of a broken heart. Please climb up!'

Templeton lay back in the straw. Lazily he placed his forepaws behind his head and crossed his knees, in an attitude of complete relaxation.

'Die of a broken heart,' he mimicked. 'How touching! My, my! I notice that it's always me you come to when in trouble. But I've never heard of anyone's heart breaking on *my* account. Oh, no. Who cares anything about old Templeton?'

'Get up!' screamed Wilbur. 'Stop acting like a spoiled child!'

Templeton grinned and lay still. 'Who made trip after trip to the dump?' he asked. 'Why, it was old Templeton! Who saved Charlotte's life by scaring that Arable boy away with a rotten goose egg? Bless my soul, I believe it was old

Templeton. Who bit your tail and got you back on your feet this morning after you had fainted in front of the crowd? Old Templeton. Has it ever occurred to you that I'm sick of running errands and doing favours? What do you think I am, anyway, a rat-of-all-work?'

Wilbur was desperate. The people were coming. And the rat was failing him. Suddenly he remembered Templeton's fondness for food.

'Templeton,' he said, 'I will make you a solemn promise. Get Charlotte's egg sac for me, and from now on I will let you eat first, when Lurvy slops me. I will let you have your choice of everything in the trough and I won't touch a thing until you're through.'

The rat sat up. 'You mean that?' he said.

'I promise. I cross my heart.'

'All right, it's a deal,' said the rat. He walked to the wall and started to climb. His stomach was still swollen from last night's gorge. Groaning and complaining, he pulled himself slowly to the ceiling. He crept along till he reached the egg sac. Charlotte moved aside for him. She was dying, but she still had strength enough to move a little. Then Templeton bared his long ugly teeth and began snipping the threads that fastened the sac to the ceiling. Wilbur watched from below.

'Use extreme care!' he said. 'I don't want a single one of those eggs harmed.'

'Thith thtuff thticks in my mouth,' complained the rat. 'It'th worth than caramel candy.'

But Templeton worked away at the job, and managed to cut the sac adrift and carry it to the ground, where he dropped it in front of Wilbur. Wilbur heaved a great sigh of relief.

'Thank you, Templeton,' he said. 'I will never forget this as long as I live.'

'Neither will I,' said the rat, picking his teeth. 'I feel as though I'd eaten a spool of thread. Well, home we go!'

Templeton crept into the crate and buried himself in the straw. He got out of sight just in time. Lurvy and John Arable and Mr Zuckerman came along at that moment, followed by Mrs Arable and Mrs Zuckerman and Avery and Fern. Wilbur had already decided how he would carry the egg sac – there was only one way possible. He carefully took the little bundle in his mouth and held it there on top of his tongue. He remembered what Charlotte had told him – that the sac was waterproof and strong. It felt funny on his tongue and made him drool a bit. And of course he couldn't say anything. But as he was being shoved into the crate, he looked up at Charlotte and gave her a wink. She knew he was saying good-bye in the only way he could. And she knew her children were safe.

'Good-bye!' she whispered. Then she summoned all her strength and waved one of her front legs at him.

She never moved again. Next day, as the Ferris wheel was being taken apart and the race horses were being loaded into vans and the entertainers were packing up their belongings and driving away in their trailers, Charlotte died. The Fair Grounds were soon deserted. The shed and buildings were empty and forlorn. The infield was littered with bottles and trash. Nobody, of the hundreds of people that had visited the Fair, knew that a grey spider had played the most important part of all. No one was with her when she died.

Chapter Twenty-Two
A Warm Wind

And so Wilbur came home to his beloved manure pile in the barn cellar. His was a strange home-coming. Around his neck he wore a medal of honour; in his mouth he held a sac of spider's eggs. There is no place like home, Wilbur thought, as he placed Charlotte's five hundred and fourteen unborn children carefully in a safe corner. The barn smelled good. His friends the sheep and the geese were glad to see him back.

The geese gave him a noisy welcome.

'Congratu-congratu-congratulations!' they cried. 'Nice work.'

Mr Zuckerman took the medal from Wilbur's

neck and hung it on a nail over the pigpen, where visitors could examine it. Wilbur himself could look at it whenever he wanted to.

In the days that followed, he was very happy. He grew to a great size. He no longer worried about being killed, for he knew that Mr Zuckerman would keep him as long as he lived. Wilbur often thought of Charlotte. A few strands of her old web still hung in the doorway. Every day Wilbur would stand and look at the torn, empty web, and a lump would come to his throat. No one had ever had such a friend – so affectionate, so loyal, and so skilful.

The autumn days grew shorter, Lurvy brought the squashes and pumpkins in from the garden and piled them on the barn floor, where they wouldn't get nipped on frosty nights. The maples and birches turned bright colours and the wind shook them and they dropped their leaves one by one to the ground. Under the wild apple trees in the pasture, the red little apples lay thick on the ground, and the sheep gnawed them and the geese gnawed them and foxes came in the night and sniffed them. One evening, just before Christmas, snow began falling. It covered house and barn and fields and woods. Wilbur had never seen snow before. When morning came he went out and ploughed the drifts in his yard, for the fun of it. Fern and Avery arrived, dragging a sledge. They coasted down the lane and out on to the frozen pond in the pasture.

'Coasting is the most fun there is,' said Avery.

'The most fun there is,' retorted Fern, 'is when the Ferris wheel stops and Henry and I are in the top car and Henry makes the car swing and we can see everything for miles and miles and miles.'

'Goodness, are you still thinking about that ol' Ferris wheel?' said Avery in disgust. 'The Fair was weeks and weeks ago.'

'I think about it all the time,' said Fern,

picking snow from her ear.

After Christmas the thermometer dropped to ten below zero. Cold settled on the world. The pasture was bleak and frozen. The cows stayed in the barn all the time now, except on sunny mornings when they went out and stood in the barnyard in the lee of the straw pile. The sheep stayed near the barn too, for protection. When they were thirsty they ate snow. The geese hung around the barnyard the way boys hang around a drug store, and Mr Zuckerman fed them corn and turnips to keep them cheerful.

'Many, many, many thanks!' they always said, when they saw food coming.

Templeton moved indoors when winter came. His ratty home under the pig trough was too chilly, so he fixed himself a cosy nest in the barn behind the grain bins. He lined it with bits of dirty newspapers and rags, and whenever he found a trinket or a keepsake he carried it home and stored it there. He continued to visit Wilbur three times a day, exactly at mealtime, and Wilbur kept the promise he had made. Wilbur let the rat eat first. Then, when Templeton couldn't hold another mouthful, Wilbur would eat. As a result of overeating, Templeton grew bigger and fatter than any rat you ever saw. He was gigantic. He was as big as a young woodchuck.

The old sheep spoke to him about his size one day. 'You would live longer,' said the old sheep, 'if you ate less.'

'Who wants to live for ever?' sneered the rat.

'I am naturally a heavy eater and I get untold satisfaction from the pleasures of the feast.' He patted his stomach, grinned at the sheep, and crept upstairs to lie down.

All winter Wilbur watched over Charlotte's egg sac as though he were guarding his own children. He had scooped out a special place in the manure for the sac, next to the board fence. On very cold nights he lay so that his breath would warm it. For Wilbur, nothing in life was so important as this small round object – nothing else mattered. Patiently he awaited the end of the winter and the coming of the little spiders. Life is always a rich and steady time when you are waiting for something to happen or to hatch. The winter ended at last.

'I heard the frogs today,' said the old sheep one evening. 'Listen! You can hear them now.'

Wilbur stood still and cocked his ears. From the pond, in shrill chorus, came the voices of hundreds of little frogs.

'Springtime,' said the old sheep, thoughtfully. 'Another spring.' As she walked away, Wilbur saw a new lamb following her. It was only a few hours old.

The snows melted and ran away. The streams and ditches bubbled and chattered with rushing water. A sparrow with a streaky breast arrived and sang. The light strengthened, the mornings came sooner. Almost every morning there was another new lamb in the sheepfold. The goose was sitting on nine eggs. The sky seemed wider and a warm wind blew. The last remaining strands of Charlotte's old web floated away and vanished.

One fine sunny morning, after breakfast, Wilbur stood watching his precious sac. He wasn't thinking of anything much. As he stood there, he noticed something move. He stepped closer and stared. A tiny spider crawled from the sac. It was no bigger than a grain of sand, no bigger than the head of a pin. Its body was grey with a black stripe underneath. Its legs were grey and tan. It looked just like Charlotte.

Wilbur trembled all over when he saw it. The little spider waved at him. Then Wilbur looked more closely. Two more little spiders crawled out and waved. They climbed round and round on the sac, exploring their new world. Then three more little spiders. Then eight. Then ten. Charlotte's children were here at last.

Wilbur's heart pounded. He began to squeal. Then he raced in circles, kicking manure into the air. Then he turned a back flip. Then he planted his front feet and came to a stop in front of Charlotte's children.

'Hello there!' he said.

The first spider said hello, but its voice was so small Wilbur couldn't hear it.

'I am an old friend of your mother's,' said Wilbur. 'I'm glad to see you. Are you all right? Is everything all right?'

The little spiders waved their forelegs at him.

Wilbur could see by the way they acted that they were glad to see him.

'Is there anything I can get you? Is there anything you need?'

The young spiders just waved. For several days and several nights they crawled here and there, up and down, around and about, waving at Wilbur, trailing tiny draglines behind them, and exploring their home. There were dozens and dozens of them. Wilbur couldn't count them, but he knew that he had a great many new friends. They grew quite rapidly. Soon each was as big as a BB shot. They made tiny webs near the sac.

Then came a quiet morning when Mr Zuckerman opened a door on the north side. A warm draught of rising air blew softly through the barn cellar. The air smelt of the damp earth, of the spruce woods, of the sweet springtime. The baby spiders felt the warm updraught. One spider climbed to the top of the fence. Then it did something that came as a great surprise to Wilbur. The spider stood on its head, pointed its spinnerets in the air, and let loose a cloud of fine silk. The silk formed a balloon. As Wilbur watched, the spider let go of the fence and rose into the air.

'Good-bye!' it said, as it sailed through the doorway.

'Wait a minute!' screamed Wilbur. 'Where do you think you're going?'

But the spider was already out of sight. Then another baby spider crawled to the top of the fence, stood on its head, made a balloon, and sailed away. Then another spider. Then another. The air was soon filled with tiny balloons, each balloon carrying a spider.

Wilbur was frantic. Charlotte's babies were disappearing at a great rate.

'Come back, children!' he cried.

'Good-bye!' they called. 'Good-bye, good-bye!'

At last one little spider took time enough to stop and talk to Wilbur before making its balloon.

'We're leaving here on the warm updraught. This is our moment for setting forth. We are aeronauts and we are going out into the world to make webs for ourselves.'

'But *where*?' asked Wilbur.

'Wherever the wind takes us. High, low. Near, far. East, west. North, south. We take to the breeze, we go as we please.'

'Are *all* of you going?' asked Wilbur. 'You can't *all* go. I would be left alone, with no friends. Your mother wouldn't want that to happen, I'm sure.'

The air was now so full of balloonists that the barn cellar looked almost as though a mist had gathered. Balloons by the dozen were rising, circling, and drifting away through the door, sailing off on the gentle wind. Cries of 'Good-bye, good-bye, good-bye!' came weakly to Wilbur's ears. He couldn't bear to watch any more. In sorrow he sank to the ground and closed his eyes. This seemed like the end of the world, to be deserted by Charlotte's children. Wilbur cried himself to sleep.

When he woke it was late afternoon. He looked at the egg sac. It was empty. He looked into the air. The balloonists were gone. Then he walked drearily to the doorway, where Charlotte's web used to be. He was standing there, thinking of her, when he heard a small voice.

'Salutations!' it said. 'I'm up here.'

'So am I,' said another tiny voice.

'So am I,' said a third voice. 'Three of us are staying. We like this place, and we like *you*.'

Wilbur looked up. At the top of the doorway three small webs were being constructed. On each web, working busily, was one of Charlotte's daughters.

'Can I take this to mean,' asked Wilbur, 'that you have definitely decided to live here in the barn cellar, and that I am going to have *three* friends?'

'You can indeed,' said the spiders.

'What are your names, please?' asked Wilbur, trembling with joy.

'I'll tell you my name,' replied the first little spider, 'if you'll tell me why you are trembling.'

'I'm trembling with joy,' said Wilbur.

'Then my name is Joy,' said the first spider.

'What was my mother's middle initial?' asked the second spider.

'A,' said Wilbur.

'Then my name is Aranea,' said the spider.

'How about me?' asked the third spider. 'Will you just pick out a nice sensible name for me –

something not too long, not too fancy, and not too dumb?'

Wilbur thought hard.

'Nellie?' he suggested.

'Fine, I like that very much,' said the third spider. 'You may call me Nellie.' She daintily fastened her orb-line to the next spoke of the web.

Wilbur's heart brimmed with happiness. He felt that he should make a short speech on this very important occasion.

'Joy! Aranea! Nellie!' he began. 'Welcome to the barn cellar. You have chosen a hallowed doorway from which to string your webs. I think it is only fair to tell you that I was devoted to your mother. I owe my very life to her. She was brilliant, beautiful, and loyal to the end. I shall always treasure her memory. To you, her daughters, I pledge my friendship, for ever and ever.'

'I pledge mine,' said Joy.

'I do, too,' said Aranea.

'And so do I,' said Nellie, who had just managed to catch a small gnat.

It was a happy day for Wilbur. And many more happy, tranquil days followed.

As time went on, and the months and years came and went, he was never without friends. Fern did not come regularly to the barn any more. She was growing up, and was careful to avoid childish things, like sitting on a milk stool near a pigpen. But Charlotte's children and grandchildren and great-grandchildren, year after year, lived in the doorway. Each spring there were new little spiders hatching out to take the place of the old. Most of them sailed away, on their balloons. But always two or three stayed and set up housekeeping in the doorway.

Mr Zuckerman took fine care of Wilbur all the rest of his days, and the pig was often visited by friends and admirers, for nobody ever forgot the year of his triumph and the miracle of the web. Life in the barn was very good – night and day, winter and summer, spring and autumn, dull days and bright days. It was the best place to be, thought Wilbur, this warm delicious cellar, with the garrulous geese, the changing seasons, the heat of the sun, the passage of swallows, the nearness of rats, the sameness of sheep, the love of spiders, the smell of manure, and the glory of everything.

Wilbur never forgot Charlotte. Although he loved her children and grandchildren dearly, none of the new spiders ever quite took her place in his heart. She was in a class by herself. It is not often that someone comes along who is a true friend and a good writer. Charlotte was both.